Other books by Fred Bonnie

Detecting Metal (Livingston Press, 1998)
Food Fights (1997)
Wide Load (1987)
Too Hot & Other Maine Stories (1987)
Displaced Persons (1983)
Squatter's Rights (1979)

*Than Ho Delivers (*2000)

Widening the ROAD

stories by

Fred Bonnie

Livingston Press
at
The University of West Alabama

ISBN 0-942979-66-4, clothbound
ISBN 0-942979-65-6, quality paper

Library of Congress CIP: 00-100413

Copyright © 2000 by Fred Bonnie

Printed in the United States of America by
Central Plains Publishing Company

Cloth binding by Heckman Bindery

Cover photo: Tricia Taylor

Proofreading: Charles Loveless, Kim Smith,
Kathleen Parnell, Amanda Snipes, Samantha
Bonnie, Pat Price, Cindy Slimp, Alan Brown,
and Patricia Taylor.

Earlier versions of several of these stories have appeared in
*The Fiddlehead, Yankee, Confrontation, and Birmingham
Magazine.*

CONTENTS

Foreword

These 15 stories have been selected from my first two collections, *Squatter's Rights* (1979) and *Displaced Persons* (1983), which were published by Oberon Press of Ottawa. When Joe Taylor, the editorial director at Livingston Press, told me he wanted to reprint both books, my first reaction was one of pride and my second was one of horror. I have come to distrust anything I wrote more than five days ago, let alone 20 years, so I've taken the liberty to revise all 15 of the stories contained herein, radically so in one or two cases. Who, given the opportunity to correct some of one's early carelessness—the sometimes sloppy work that results from a youthful rush to publish—would ignore such a second chance to impose minor improvement on one's early stories?

Ultimately, then, this edition is not a re-release of my first two books; it is a different book, re-seen through the eyes of 20 additional years of reading, writing, and study of craft. Two stories, "The Ark Rested in the Seventh Month" (from *Squatter's Rights*) and "The Hunting Season" (from *Displaced Persons*) did not, for a variety of reasons, make the cut. Hence the new title for the regrouping of these stories.

I owe thanks to many people—to Joe Taylor at Livingston Press for republishing these stories in the United States; to Dilshad Macklem, my editor at Oberon Press in Canada, for publishing them in their original forms in Canada; to my daughter Samantha and to Pat Price for their help in preparing the manuscript; to Buddy Colvin, head cheerleader in all my writing efforts. Thanks also for encouragement early on from Burt Caldwell, Chris Keith, Derrick Semler, and Reno T. Simone. Finally, I wish to raise a glass to the memory of Jesse Hill Ford; Fr. Joseph "The Owl" Mahoney, SJ; and to the late Jane Fox.

August 1999
Columbiana

Widening
the
ROAD

For Gene Yarrington and Chip Skoglund

Squatter's Rights

As Lloyd was heating water for tea with his lunch, he heard voices outside his cabin and went to the door, which he had left ajar. Two men, one of them his son-in-law, Gordon Burgess, stood in front of the old black Chevy sedan that had been parked by the cabin for seven years. Gordon glanced toward the cabin door, saw the old man peeking, and looked away. Lloyd watched as Gordon fished in his pocket.

"I got the key in here somewheres...."

"You mean this thing runs," the other man chided.

Gordon said nothing. He opened the door and slid in.

The car started effortlessly, as if merely sitting behind the wheel were enough to spark the ignition. Gordon got out, and both men stepped back from the car. It was covered with leaves, both left-side tires were flat, but the engine hummed evenly, almost soundlessly.

"Don't sound bad," the visitor said.

Lloyd looked on through the partly open door, but when the visitor looked up and noticed him, Lloyd pushed the door shut but continued to listen.

"Mornin', Lloyd," the visitor hollered.

Gordon raised the hood, and the leaves gathered in a small pile on the windshield. "This oil ain't been changed in two, three years and look at it. Still yellow." He pulled out the dipstick for Sid to see.

"How about those tires, though, Gordon? You gonna put a couple new tires on the front for me?"

"Hadn't planned on it."

"Well now, I can't very well buy it if I can't even drive it home, can I?"

"Then, go get some tires," Gordon suggested. "I'll help you put them on."

1

"That ain't the point, Gordon." Sid scratched the back of his neck. "The point is I don't feel like forking out money for a pair of tires."

Both men were silent for a moment. Sid could not keep himself from glancing over his shoulder at the cabin.

"Say, Gordon, the old man getting a little loose in his old age?"

"No worse than ever."

"What does he do with himself all day?"

"I dunno," Gordon said, his eyes locked on the car. "Just sets, I guess."

Lloyd backed away from the door and took a rusted double-barrelled shotgun out of a wall cabinet. He opened the breach and stuffed a plastic pill vial into one of the barrels, then shut it again.

"Hey, Lloyd," he heard Sid holler. "Come on out and say hello. Ain't seen you in five, ten years."

Lloyd slid along the wall to the window and peeped outside until Sid turned back to the car. Then Lloyd raised the shotgun and took aim. *Bam*, he whispered. He lowered the gun and watched as the two men shut the hood and sauntered to Gordon's pickup. When they were gone, Lloyd went out to inspect the car, shotgun still in hand. What could he take, he wondered, to make it hard for them to drive that car off. A few spark plugs? But Gordon would surely have extra spark plugs right up there in the barn. And if not, he could always get some at a filling station. But a missing distributor cap might hold things up just about right. Gordon would have to look around a little harder to find a 1949 Chevy distributor cap.

Lloyd smiled. And after that, Gordon could spend a day or two looking for a generator, too. . . .

*****

Gordon and Sid came back after lunch carrying tires, windshield wiper blades and a seat cover. Lloyd watched through a peephole he had drilled in the door for the occasion. By the time they had changed the tires, Lloyd's clock said ten after two. The sky had begun to darken, and when he wasn't watching Gordon and Sid, Lloyd watched the spasms of breeze lift the leaves from the car, hold them for a moment, then twist them away.

"Looks like we're gonna get that storm they was talking about on the radio," Sid said gravely.

"Ay-uh." Gordon slid behind the wheel and tried to start the car, but no sound came when he turned the key.

"What's the matter?" Sid asked.

Gordon lifted the hood and his eyes roamed over the engine. "That old bastard," he muttered. He turned toward the cabin. "Okay Lloyd, you can bring that generator and distributor cap out any time. And anything else you took."

Lloyd smiled but did not answer.

"Damn it, you bring that stuff out here!"

"Threw it out," Lloyd hollered through the barred door. "Distributor cap warn't no good. All coated with cow dung."

Gordon and Sid looked at each other. "Just bring it out," Gordon hollered. "We'll worry about the cowshit some other time."

"Too late now," Lloyd said. "Used it for fertilizer."

Gordon strode onto the porch and tried to open the door. "C'mon, Lloyd. This ain't the time for games."

Lloyd's voice rose high and strained. "Well now, if you'd asked me one time what I thought about you selling my car, maybe we wouldn't be playing them."

"That car happens to be mine," Gordon said, his eyes focused on the door latch. "You ain't driven it in ten years."

"I asked you over eight years ago for that car and you didn't say no. It's mine now. Been here over seven years. Squatter's rights."

"Well, let me inside. We can talk about it."

"It ain't for sale. There ain't nothing to talk about."

"Don't forget," Gordon said, lowering his voice, "the court appointed Bertha and me to be your legal guardians. I wouldn't have to ask your permission to sell that car, even if it *was* yours. Which it ain't."

"That car ain't gettin' sold," Lloyd said.

Gordon waited a moment before taking up the challenge. "It ain't, huh? We'll see." He came back to the car where Sid waited. "Look, Joe Duffy's got a junk Chevy over in his dooryard. I'll just zip over there and get the distributor cap and generator off'n it. You stay here and make sure he don't do nothing else to that car."

Sid sighed and tapped his fingers on the fender. "I ain't got all afternoon, Gordon. This storm's comin in fast...."

"I'll be back in a few minutes," Gordon said. He stuffed his pipe into his breast pocket and started toward his pickup.

Sid turned back toward the cabin, glancing between the two

front windows.

"Whatcha been up to, Lloyd?" he hollered. When no answer came, Sid opened the car door and got in. He looked up at the cabin again and saw half of Lloyd's face peering out at him, the other half hidden by the window frame. Sid waved once, but Lloyd neither waved back nor moved; he kept only half his face visible and pressed against the pane. Sid breathed on the windshield to fog it up, since Lloyd continued to stare.

"Oil in that block might be yellow," Lloyd hollered. "So's the gas in the tank. And I'll tell you just exactly how it got that way, if you want to know."

*****

By the time Gordon got back with the distributor cap, it was nearly four. Sid leaned against the fender and watched him work. Gordon cussed the wind as it blew his hair in his face and leaves onto his hands.

"I thought you said the oil in this thing was changed two years ago."

"That's right."

"Well...what's the old man saying...you just changed it this morning?"

"You been talking to him while I was gone?"

Sid watched without speaking for a few minutes more, glancing from time to time at the door of the cabin when it rattled in the stronger gusts.

"Gordon, you sure you didn't change that oil just this morning before I came out?"

Gordon looked up. "You calling me a friggin' liar?"

"No, I was just wondering. Man's got a right to wonder."

Gordon stood up from under the hood and held the wrench toward Sid. "Look, you can put your own generator on."

Sid looked at the wrench but didn't take it. "I didn't mean nothing by that, Gordon. Man's got a right to wonder...."

"Not out loud." Gordon bent over the engine again. Neither man spoke until Gordon gave his wrench a final twist and stepped back from the car.

"Start her up," he ordered.

Sid got in and turned the key. The motor churned but wouldn't start. Gordon's eyes crawled over the engine from the radiator cap to the windshield wipers.

"Hey, Sid," the old man hollered from inside the cabin. "You want to buy something that don't even start?"

Sid got out of the car. He looked at Gordon and then at the cabin. "It started okay this morning, Lloyd, and it'd prob'ly be okay now if you hadn't been messing with it."

"Yeah, but how do you know I ain't done something beyond fixing?"

"Don't listen to him," Gordon warned, pointing toward the cabin with his wrench.

"...Like, how do you know I ain't dumped a little sawdust into the gas tank?"

Sid looked automatically toward the gas cap, then down at the ground.

"Don't listen to him. You listen to him and that makes you as crazy as him."

Sid pointed at the sawdust leavings on the ground. "Look at that."

Gordon shrugged. "He probably sprinkled it there just so's you'd *think* he done something more." The hesitation grew on Sid's face.

"Course it depends," Lloyd hollered, "on just what you're lookin' for in a car. Now if you just want somethin' to *set* in, this one might do. But if you're looking for something to drive, I'd look somewheres else."

"You ain't gonna believe him, are you?" Gordon pressed.

"How much you paying for it?" Lloyd asked.

"A hundred."

Lloyd laughed. "Offer him ten."

Sid looked pained.

"Awwww, go on," Gordon said disgustedly. "If you're gonna believe that old bastard, you're as crazy as he is."

Sid shuffled nervously, looking up at the sky. "Look, I gotta get back and get my cows in. We can talk about it tomorrow, after the storm."

"Awww...."

"We'll see you later...."

"Hold on a minute there, Sid. I just spent two dollars on a distributor cap and five for a generator for this thing. I figure you owe me seven bucks."

Sid's eyes weighed the situation. "Okay," he said, reaching for his wallet. "But I'll want to take that distributor cap and generator along with me. I'll be back tomorrow after the storm to get 'em."

*****

As soon as they were gone, Lloyd went out to replace the distributor cap and generator, plus the coil and several worthless spark plugs he'd found in his medicine cabinet. A light rain had begun, and the wind blew in wet slaps around his face. After he studied the wires under the dashboard and remembered which ones to cross, the car started easily. He wanted to leave right away, but he knew he would have to wait until nightfall to get by Gordon. He went into the cabin and began to pack. He didn't plan to take much with him: two shirts, a radio that needed batteries, all seventeen pairs of socks that he owned, four sets of long underwear—the only kind he had ever worn, regardless of the season. He also brought two five hundred-dollar savings bonds, which comprised his life savings, plus his old shotgun. The more he looked around the cabin, the more things he saw that he wanted to bring along. He piled things on the back seat of the car: clothes, tools, old magazines, a zither with no strings.

He thought of Gordon and how upset he would be that the car was gone, but happy enough to be rid of Lloyd that he would not come after it. Lloyd would be happy to be rid of Gordon and his attempts to force Lloyd into a nursing home. Lloyd had refused to talk about it—had even threatened to burn the house down if Gordon and Bertha ever brought it up again. The next day he'd moved his things out of the big house and into the cabin he had built for himself back when Gordon and Bertha were first married—built it, he said at the time, for his old age. Lloyd had not realized that old age was upon him until the first time the topic of a nursing home arose.

The black Chevy had been abandoned by the cabin even before Lloyd moved in.

He made a stew from leftovers in the refrigerator and ate, still thinking about Gordon and how they had argued from the beginning. Gordon had come one day to see about a tractor Lloyd had for sale, and Gordon argued with him about the horsepower. He didn't buy the tractor, but he was back the next month when Lloyd had a horse for sale. That was the first time Gordon saw Bertha. After that, Gordon started coming by once or twice a week for eggs. Bertha was flirtatious—embarrassingly so, Lloyd had always thought—and although she wasn't really buxom, she knew how to hold her shoulders so that she seemed so. She was nineteen and Gordon was thirty-two when they got married. Within a year Gordon bought the farm that Lloyd had leased for more than thirty years but had never been able to buy. Now

Gordon milked forty head, kept two thousand hens, and owned almost three hundred acres of land. He did not need a nineteen-forty-nine Chevrolet fishtail-back sedan. Especially when Lloyd, not Gordon Burgess, was the rightful owner.

*****

The wind whistled over the chimney and shook the windows. Lloyd had always loved a hard storm and now he listened for a while, jumping with each clap of thunder, especially those that quickly followed the bright, sizzling flashes of lightning. He glanced around the lamp-lit cabin where he'd lived these seven years, hoping that Gordon and Bertha had lost their electricity by now. Big Bertha, his wife, had always hated an electrical storm, but Lloyd had long considered a thunderstorm a sign to act on something important. There was a storm the day that Big Bertha died, and Lloyd decided between burial and cremation. He would have buried her if the funeral home had been willing to put her under in a plastic bag or, better, a cardboard box. But he wasn't about to spend several thousand dollars on a casket.

When Lloyd thought it was dark enough for him to get by the house, he walked to the loaded car—slowly, as if the sun were shining. The rain pelted him, the droplets running up and across his face rather than down. His clothes were soaked by the time he got into the car, which started with the first tiny twist of the key.

He drove with the lights out, easing along the muddy cow path. The rain pelted the windshield so hard that Lloyd had to roll down the window and stick his head out to see as he drove. He could hear nothing above the blasts of wind, and he reached the paved road sooner than he'd expected. A few hundred yards beyond the house, he turned on the headlights, rolled the window up, and dried his face and hair with one of his spare shirts.

He figured the hard part was over.

He knew he had to go south to get to Florida, so he headed south. On the open road, the wind grappled with the car. He drove slowly, neck painfully craned forward, hands tense and tired as he gripped the steering-wheel. The twisting rain obliterated the lane markings in the road, slowing him to about ten miles an hour. He had never liked to drive and hadn't really expected ever to have to drive again. The few friends he had came to see him once every year or two, and that was all the sociability he wanted. Any more than a few people at a time made him nervous. Little Bertha made him nervous, too, when she came to

sit and talk about the curtains she was going to make for him
and the braided rug she'd been working on for over a year. Bertha had evolved from almost buxom to card-carrying plump in
eighteen years of childless marriage. It was a fitting revenge, Lloyd
had decided, for everything good that had ever happened to Gordon Burgess.

The driving was a little easier on the main road, which was
wider and where the lane markings were visible, although just
barely. When he rolled up his window, the hiss of the tires on
the flowing pavement pleasantly blended with the noises of the
car—the rattles from under the dashboard, the creak of the
springs, the tinkling of the warped blade in the heater fan, the
squeal of the speedometer, which Lloyd could not explain. It was,
he realized with a smile, the first time he'd ever driven this car,
although he'd long considered it his.

He turned on the radio and listened to the static, the only
sound since he'd broken off the antenna one night when he was
mad at Gordon and Bertha—the night of the first nursing home
discussion, he remembered now.

Lloyd hit a deep rut, and the impact jarred the hood latch
loose. The hood rose up, hesitated a moment, then snapped off
its hinges and clattered over the roof into the road behind him.
He wasn't sure what to do, so he pulled over to the side of the
road. The next gust of wind tossed the hood into the gully. In
moments the engine stalled. Lloyd twisted the key again and
again, but he couldn't get the car started. The rain battered the
roof and swept in a thick film down the windshield. He opened
the window and stuck his head out. At first the rain felt good
against his face, collecting in his week-old whiskers. But as the
water began to run down his neck, he got a chill and rolled his
window up again.

He would just have to wait out the storm, he decided. If his
hood wasn't too badly damaged, he'd get it reattached and continue on to Florida in the morning. He wished he had batteries
for his portable radio, and that the good radio shows, like Jack
Benny, were still on. He remembered packing some cans of sardines and began to search for them. He had brought a box of
crackers, too, and apples from the tree behind his cabin. He ate
two cans of sardines, then waited a while before eating an apple.

While he smoked a cigarette, he thought he saw headlights in
the thick rain on his windshield. The car pulled alongside, and
Lloyd saw that it was a police cruiser. The cop inside looked at

Lloyd, then backed up and pulled in behind the old Chevy. Lloyd
rolled his window tight and locked all the doors. In a moment
the officer tapped with his flashlight on the window. Lloyd stared
straight ahead.

"Hey in there, you all right?" the cop hollered over the whistling wind.

Lloyd nodded, but said nothing.

"You got new plates for this vehicle?" the officer asked.

Lloyd didn't answer.

After a few moments, the cop once again tapped with his flashlight. "Get out your license and registration and come on back
to my car."

"Left them at home," Lloyd said.

The officer's powerful flashlight roamed over the car, hover-
ing for a moment over the exposed engine, then beaming directly
in on Lloyd.

"The plates on this vehicle expired seven years ago." He tried
to open Lloyd's door, then the back door. "Open up."

Lloyd stared straight ahead.

"This is no time for games, old fella."

Lloyd made no move to open the door and continued to stare
straight ahead. The officer went back to his car and turned on
the blue light. Lloyd watched the light swirl in his rearview mirror. He tried to start the car again, but everything was too wet.
In a few minutes the flashlight tapped again.

"Are you Gordon Burgess?"

By instinct Lloyd shook his head.

"Then who are you?"

Lloyd silently glared at his windshield.

"Look fella, I could arrest you right now for driving an un-
registered, uninspected vehicle, probably driving without a license, refusing to cooperate with an officer, and parking so as to
obstruct a throughway. And if you don't open the door and tell
me who you are, I'm adding resisting arrest and stealing a car to
the list."

"This is my car," Lloyd jumped, turning to face the man.

"The last registration on this car was under the name Gordon Burgess. If that isn't you, you're liable for car theft."

"Okay, okay, I'm Gordon Burgess." Lloyd swallowed hard
as he said it.

"I think you're lying," the officer said.

"Why don't you go prevent a murder some place and leave

me the hell alone!" Lloyd shouted into the beam of the flash-light. The officer said nothing and went back to his car. At first Lloyd thought he was going to leave, but he didn't. The blue light continued to churn through the thick rain on Lloyd's back window.

When Lloyd saw a new set of headlights approaching, he knew it was Gordon. Lloyd tried the engine again. He looked at the back seat piled high with his things, blaming his possessions for the engine failure. Then Gordon and the officer were at his window.

"Open it up, Lloyd. Before you get in any more trouble than you're already in."

"Leave me alone."

"Want me to press charges against you for car theft?"

"Go ahead, if you want to look foolish. It's my car."

Gordon took out his key and fumbled with it, inserting it finally in the lock, but Lloyd pressed with the bottom of his fist on the inside lock button. The button strained but did not come up. Gordon took the key out and ran to the other side of the car, but Lloyd held that button down, too.

Gordon cussed, then said to the officer, "Come here a minute."

Lloyd watched them go to the back of the Chevy and crouch out of sight behind it. Lloyd slid to the middle of the seat and stretched his arms to reach both lock buttons. He was able to reach them with his fingertips, but not with his fists. Instead, he lay on his back across the seat and held one button with his heel and the other with his hands. There were no exterior locks on the back doors. As he had suspected, they came to both sides of the car and both had keys, though only one, Lloyd figured, was the real Chevy key. They stayed crouched out of sight, but Lloyd knew Gordon was on the driver's side; he could feel him through the door.

The real key was on the other side, he could tell in his heel. He sprang to it with both hands, realizing he was staking every-thing on Gordon's having only one key to the Chevy. The of-ficer turned hard—Lloyd could feel it as he mashed down with both fists—but Lloyd summoned all his strength, and after a long, strained moment, the officer's key snapped off inside the lock.

"Oh no," Gordon groaned. "Shit shit shit!" He grabbed the door handle and rocked the car. "So help me, I'll take that door right off the hinges if you don't open up."

Lloyd plugged his ears and stared straight ahead.

Gordon and the officer went back to the patrol car. The inside light was on. In the subsiding rain, Lloyd could see them talking. He waited for them to come back but they didn't. He decided to eat some more sardines and crackers. As he ate, he kept a constant eye on the patrol car. The officer was a good twenty.years younger than Gordon, Lloyd figured.

When they did return, Gordon seemed calmer and stood with his hands in his pockets. The officer trained his flashlight on Lloyd and said nothing.

"I'm trying to work out a deal for you," Gordon said. "This man here is pretty upset with you, and I don't blame him a bit. Now he's suggesting that if we take you home and come back some other day to get the car, he'll forget he ever laid eyes on you. But if you don't cut this nonsense out, he's charging you with car theft and a bunch of other stuff."

Lloyd stared straight ahead, watching the windshield wipers where they had frozen in mid-act. Without the heater, the car was cold.

"We'll give you two minutes to decide, Lloyd. Just come on over and get in the cruiser when you're ready."

They went back to the patrol car. The officer turned off his blue light and turned on the yellow flashers. The two minutes went by as Lloyd counted silently to one hundred and twenty, then waited for the yellow flashers to go off and the blue light to come back on. He noticed that the rain had let up but the wind still shook the car from time to time. He tried to start the engine once more.

A new flashing yellow light appeared in the mirror, and a wrecker pulled up to the patrol car. Lloyd saw Gordon motion with his thumb at the Chevy. Lloyd sat straight up as the wrecker pulled in front of him, then backed up quickly. Lloyd grabbed the steering wheel to brace himself, but the wrecker did not ram him. He looked in the mirror and saw that Gordon and the officer were still in the patrol car.

The wrecker operator jumped out and disappeared under the front of Lloyd's car. Lloyd heard the chains latch like handcuffs onto the front end. Moments later, the winch jerked the front of the car off the ground. Through his windshield Lloyd could see only the top of the winch. The operator unhooked the linkage arm from the shifting lever to disengage the gears. Lloyd yanked at the handbrake but remembered the cable had rotted out years before.

The wrecker lurched forward, and Lloyd wrenched the steering wheel from side to side. Behind them followed the police car with its blue light on as well as its yellow emergency flashers. Behind the cruiser came Gordon. Each time they went through a rut, the car swayed precariously, and Lloyd hugged the steering wheel. He figured he was being hauled to jail, but at the first filling station they came to, the wrecker made a U-turn and headed back toward Morrisville. Of course, Lloyd thought; they would put him in jail in Morrisville, not Bangor.

But they passed through the town and headed out the road toward Gordon's farm rather than turn left to go toward the town hall, two rooms of which had bars on the windows and were used for a jail. The wind was more even now, though still strong, and the rain had nearly stopped. Here and there a tree had been blown over, and there were new ruts in the road where the water had collected. They met two other cars on the outskirts of town, and both pulled over to let the procession by, gaping at Lloyd as he glared back at them.

At Gordon's road they stopped. All the flashing lights went off, and the cruiser backed around and left them. Gordon got out of his car and paid the wrecker operator. Lloyd squinted, trying to see how much. When the wrecker moved again, Gordon didn't follow. He went, instead, up the hill to his house.

The wrecker towed Lloyd to his cabin and set him down in what Lloyd considered the wrong place. He rolled down the window as the operator got out.

"Hey, would you set it down over there?"

The operator looked annoyed. "Come on man...."

"Look, I'll pay you. You can have the battery out of this thing. And any other parts you want."

The operator glanced at the exposed engine. "That battery ain't worth the powder to blow it to hell." He sighed and got back into the wrecker. "Hold on."

He set the Chevy down more or less exactly where Lloyd wanted it. The sun was beginning to come up, buried deep in the clouds. Lloyd watched how fast the sky moved in the wind.

He waved at the wrecker as it pulled away, and the operator waved back. Lloyd rummaged in the back seat for blankets and a pillow, then settled himself in the front seat to sleep. He closed his eyes, but only for a moment. He sat back up and looked outside, a bit irked as he realized that the wrecker had not set the car down exactly where it had been.

Fifty Winters

Usually, when he got to our house, I was just getting up. He'd look at me with his stiff, chilly grin while he placed the frosty milk bottles on the counter, look away still grinning and, between the bottles, look at his watch, a drop of ice from his white beard melting onto the sleeve of his jacket.

"Son of a gun," he'd say, as if to himself. "I didn't realize it was so late." And he'd look back at me again. My brother McLeod, seven years old then, always came out to watch, standing nearly naked in the middle of the cold kitchen floor, sometimes with as much as one sock on, sometimes even an untied shoe and in one leg of his longjohns (not necessarily the same side as the shoe), edging nearer the stove but never taking his eyes off the hands that whisked the bottles from the wire carrier to the counter—the wire carrier that steamed from the heat of the room on mornings when it was really cold.

And as if the stiff, cracked hands that yet were so incongruously supple knew they were being watched, they would suddenly stretch like tentacles and pull out three bottles at once. McLeod would watch, but his face showed no amazement. Only if you knew him well did you understand how amazed he really was. Then the milkman's fingers would reach out for four bottles. Still no change in McLeod's expression as he glanced from me to the milkman to the other leg of his longjohns, which he carried in his hand with a maddening nonchalance.

"What does the teacher say when you come to school dressed like that?"

McLeod never seemed to understand.

"Well, I gotta get going. Cold one, huh?" And he'd chide me with his smile again.... "Oh, that's right...you ain't been out yet. I guess you wouldn't know if it was ninety, would you? You just got up."

He'd have this cold hand around my biceps, exerting enough pressure so that if I didn't flex my muscle it would hurt.

"You sure you don't want some coffee, Moses?" Dad would say.

But Moses seldom took coffee.

"God, no. I'm way behind already." He'd tighten his grip on my arm and nod. "Give it to this one here. He needs it worse than I do."

I'd take the pressure on my arm as long as I could, then give up. "Ow, okay, okay. You win."

He'd let go of my arm then, take his carrier from the counter, and poke McLeod's stomach on his way out the door.

Even five or ten minutes after he'd left, the room stayed filled with his presence. At least until the wet tracks on the floor had dried.

*****

I used to go with him most Saturday mornings. It wasn't so much that he needed my help, he just wanted the company, I suspected. I'd go to bed on the couch downstairs on Friday night, and he'd come in quietly and stand over me like a shadow, prodding at my feet with the cold, metal bottle carrier.

"Hey! Jeffery! Come on. It's five already."

I was a slow waker, even after I'd managed to stand up. He'd watch me pull on my trousers as if he were supervising the operation. Then for the choice of jackets.

"Is it cold?" I'd ask.

"Of course."

In the truck, which he'd have already loaded before coming to get me, he would have coffee heating on a little sterno burner. And doughnuts. The cab of the truck was an island of warmth and light in the cold morning air.

The morning I remember most vividly, it was snowing harder than usual—heavy, wet snow that stuck to the truck's tires and compressed itself into ice almost as quickly as it touched down. Moses never wore gloves, but that morning he kept his hands in his pockets when he wasn't using them. He'd turned off the windshield wipers while the truck was idle and we drank our coffee. The snow on the windshield seemed like a wall that might collapse on us.

"It's going to be a slow day," Moses half whistled to himself.

"Is it really slippery?"

"Yep. Worse it's been this winter, anyway." He stared ahead, as if he could see through the windshield. I sensed that he wanted to get going.

"Have some more coffee, Mose."

"No, thanks. Had too much already."

I finished mine as quickly as I could without scalding my throat. Moses wasn't one to tell you not to hurry when that wasn't the way he felt. As I was draining the last from my cup, he pumped down the clutch pedal and yanked the shift lever into first. I was always amazed watching Moses—and the other milkmen, for that matter—drive those old Divco trucks standing up. The wipers came on and instantly created two fan shaped windows to the outside. The truck slowly lunged ahead into the powerful beams of the headlights.

The milk went off quickly enough in town, but when we got out toward the lake where the stops were half a mile or more apart, the pace was tedious. On the flat straight-aways it was just a question of patience. But on the hills, especially going down, it was not so easy and, without looking directly at Moses, I could sense the tenseness on his face. It was unlike him to say so little. He usually had lots of stories, either about the people on the route, or about the one great adventure of his life—his two years in the army, first in Norway, then in Hawaii. He got discharged two weeks before the Japanese attacked Pearl Harbor. When I asked him once what he'd liked best about the army, he answered without hesitation.

"Getting up early."

By five-thirty we started meeting snowplows. All the drivers knew Moses, and they all waved. Moses loosened up a little and talked for a while, mostly ribbing me for not having a girlfriend yet. I did have one, in fact, but I wasn't about to tell Moses about her. I'd once mentioned a girl I was interested in, and Moses urged me to start lifting weights and getting in better shape—it took some good-looking muscles to get a girl nowadays, he said. Dad had observed to me more than once that the older Moses got, the more he teased everyone younger than he about things like strength and stamina.

"You know," Moses said, interrupting my thoughts, "if the plow has been out on the Moose Pond Road, we'll be all set." He winked, as he did at least fifty times a day, but he looked away quickly, directing his attention back to the road. I watched him as he stood stiffly at the wheel, the crow's feet at the corners of his eyes deepening by the minute. It occurred to me that I'd never seen him worried.

When we got to Moose Pond Road, it was nearly seven, and the road had not been plowed. We stopped to have another cup of coffee. Moses shut off the wipers, and in seconds we were once more isolated from the world.

"He'll be along in a few minutes," Moses thought aloud.

"We could do a couple hours down Highland Road and come back."

"No," he said solemnly. "The Harpers, the Miltons and the Clearys have all got small kids. They'll be waiting for milk."

Moses watched his side-view mirror while he drank. I watched the steam rise from my cup when I wasn't wolfing doughnuts. Moose Pond Road lay to the left of the truck, disappearing into the snow and the woods. After I finished a fourth doughnut, Moses, as if suddenly awakened from a dream, turned on the wipers and put the truck in gear.

"Heck, Mose, they can wait a couple hours; even with little kids."

"We can start. Plow'll be along in a few minutes. Then we'll just follow him."

"I think you're crazy...."

"Look, youngster," he snapped, "you don't want to come, fine. But you better be careful who you call crazy. I'm not one of you young loafers with nothing better to do but play basketball all afternoon."

I felt my mouth open with surprise. I even thought, for a second, that I was going to cry. "I'm sorry, Mose...I..."

"You with me or not?"

"Of course. I just thought it would be better if we waited."

"Well, we're already an hour late. It's seven o'clock. We can't wait any longer."

His voice had become less angered. I figured he felt bad about speaking sharply to me, though I didn't expect him to apologize; that wouldn't have been his style. His style was to just bull ahead, whether it made sense or not. I couldn't help but picture us sliding off the road into some massive snowbank that six plow trucks couldn't pull us out of.

The first hill wasn't too bad. When the truck hesitated near the top, it was only long enough for the chains to bite down through the snow until they found something solid to dig into. Going down the other side, Moses kept the truck in low gear, and we inched down the hill like a caterpillar on a cornstalk.

The snow blew furiously at us as if we'd done something to provoke it. Each time we skidded or swayed, the cases of milk bumped around in the back of the truck. It occurred to me that the only thing separating about a ton of milk from the cab was a canvas curtain.

Moses seemed less irritable. "There's chocolate milk in back there," he said.

"No, thanks."

"Well, why don't you eat those doughnuts up? There's more in the egg cabinet."

"No, thanks. I'm not hungry."

I watched him out of the corner of my eye, saw the splotchy, parched hands that gripped the steering wheel so tightly they were blue. The headlight beams quivered out over the snow like divining rods as his tightly squinted eyes struggled to distinguish white road from white non-road. Whenever we stopped to make a delivery, Moses seemed to go limp, like a deflated balloon, and he'd get his smile back for a few minutes.

At the Harper house, two of the kids came out to the road to meet the truck. Moses and I loaded their arms, as if the milk bottles were birch logs.

"Hello there, Moses!" Mrs. Harper's form in the doorway was barely discernible in the swirling snow.

"Mornin', Helen. You order this?"

"Yes sir, Moses. Just for you."

"Well, it's good to know I've got friends."

He laughed as the children squeezed by with the milk. "Thanks a million, Moses. We ran out of milk last night. The station wagon would never have made it through this."

"Nothing to it, Helen. See you Tuesday."

"You sure you don't want some coffee?"

"Ain't got time, but thanks just the same."

We pulled slowly along. I waited for Moses to give me the "I-told-you-so" grin, but he was already busy again watching the road. By the time we got to the Eldred place, it was seven-thirty and still dark out. I ran up to the porch with the milk, and Sam Eldred was there waiting.

"You're a life saver," he said. "We didn't have a drop left in the house."

Moses hollered from the truck. "How come you don't have the woman out shoveling yet, Sam?"

Sam stood there shivering in his bathrobe. "Waiting for it to pile up, Mose. Give her a better workout. You fellas like some coffee?"

"Can't, we're late."

"Well, you be careful this morning, Mose. It looks pretty bad." Sam waved and disappeared inside.

We emerged from the woods and started to climb into the clear, open area that was called Crescent Hill. The wind lashed viciously at the truck, which was no longer sheltered by the trees, and we fish-tailed our way up the hill. It was starting to get light out.

At the crest of the hill, Moses stopped the truck. I wondered if he had decided to wait for the plow truck after all, but I was wrong.

"Open your door," he said.

I looked at him for a second, then did as he had ordered. The wind entered the truck like a mad landlord, and I tucked my neck as far into my coat as I could. Before us stretched the steep road that the wind had swept free of snow, leaving only ice. At the bottom of the hill was the brook, indistinguishable under ice and snow, and the narrow, wooden-railed bridge.

"You ready?" he asked.

I wanted to mention once again that we might want to wait until the plow came through to salt and sand the road, but I said nothing. I felt the truck inch forward.

"Look, Moses, can I shut this door? I'm freezing."

"Leave it open until we get to the bottom."

He grasped the wheel and eased the truck down the treacherous hill. He kept the front and rear wheels on the right side in the snow bank. I imagined that we were parachuting in slow motion down the hill, the speedometer not even flickering from zero. I wondered if we were moving at all.

Then we drifted just a few inches back out onto the road, skidding on the ice that was hidden under the light glaze of snow. We began to careen back and forth between the two snow banks whose cores had been hardening all winter long. Each hard bump against the banks sent the milk cases in back thudding against the walls. I could feel us going into an uncontrolled slide down the hill, slowly at first, then picking up speed. The truck slowly turned, the next thing I knew we were hurtling down the hill backward.

Moses wrenched the steering wheel from side to side, the sweat loose on his forehead and cheeks, as if it had been waiting just under the skin all morning.

"Jump!" Moses shouted. I froze. He waited only a second, then shoved me through the open door. I landed on the hard, icy road and rolled over and over, sliding down the hill and into the snow bank. I sat up just in time to see the truck veer off the road, up over the snow bank into the field, and then roll over twice in an explosion of breaking glass. The truck came to a rest on its side.

I ran the rest of the way down the hill, slipping, falling, bounding over the banking into the thigh-deep snow. Moses had been thrown from the truck and lay face down in the snow, whimpering like a puppy.

"Moses, are you all right? Answer me, Moses!"

Out of the corner of my eye I saw the flashing yellow light of the plow truck. It rumbled to a halt, and the driver leaped out and ran toward us.

"Look out!" I heard myself holler. "There's glass everywhere!"

*****

The plow driver radioed for an ambulance, which arrived in a surprisingly short time. They took Moses to the hospital, even though he insisted he was all right.

"Internal injuries," they told him. "You can never tell...."

So Moses sat in an emergency room bed, protesting loudly whenever a nurse tried to examine him.

"Does it hurt here? No? How about here?"

"I've told you it doesn't hurt anywhere."

Finally, Dr. Russell arrived and persuaded Moses to take a sleeping pill and rest. The doctor asked me for details about the crash, and I told him as much as I could recall. But the whole thing had become little more than a terrifying blur to me. I was still trembling, hours later. I told the doctor I was amazed that Moses was still alive.

The next day was Sunday, and I went to visit Moses in the afternoon. It had stopped snowing sometime early Sunday morning, the plows had been going non-stop for twelve hours or more, and the hospital parking-lot was black and bare and wet. There were visitors in his room, people from the route, and Moses sat up in bed complaining that he was perfectly all right, and still they wouldn't let him go home. He massaged his hands constantly, first the right with the left, then vice-versa. I didn't stay very long.

Monday afternoon, after school, I came back again. The door

to his room was slightly ajar and I stepped in quietly. Moses was sitting up, sleeping with his chin on his chest. I imagined that he'd refused, on principle, to lie down. At the foot of the bed a TV mumbled softly to itself. Various tags hanging from the many flower vases read, "From the folks on Maple Street," "The Folks on Grove Point," "Your friends on Ralston Road."

I wondered if I shouldn't have come back in an hour or so, but as I started out the door, Moses' head jerked up, and he blinked at me.

"Thought I heard someone." He waved impatiently at the TV. "That foolish thing. Turn it off, would you? Drives me batty."

I turned it off and caught him studying me. "You all right?" he asked.

"Yeah. I'm okay. Little stiff and sore in places."

"When they letting you out?"

He was working his hands again, more vigorously than before. "I dunno. I never felt better, but they gotta run all these foolish tests."

He asked about the condition of the truck and who had finished the route, then he shook his head slowly. "Lost a lot of milk. A lot of milk...."

Tuesday afternoon when I got there, Moses was awake and actually watching the television, though he pretended he wasn't.

"They say when they might let you out?"

"Doctor says tomorrow." He still worked his hands, squeezing, rubbing them, bending his fingers backward and forward. "I'm going to go buggy if I have to stay here much longer."

"You must have some sick leave or something coming, don't you?"

"Yeah, I guess so." He seemed suddenly embarrassed. "It ain't that, though...." He seemed to be fumbling in his head for just exactly what it was. "Hell," he said finally, "I ain't missed a day of work in seventeen years."

I remembered a question I'd always wanted to ask but never had. "How long have you been a milkman, anyway, Mose?"

He looked around as if someone might be listening. When he spoke, it was in a whisper. "Fifty years or so."

The next day I had debate club after school. Moses had said the day before that he was going home, so I didn't stop at the hospital. It occurred to me that I had no idea where he lived.

The day after that, as I passed the hospital on my way home from school, I got a strange feeling, kind of a ripple of nausea that lasted just a few seconds. I got nearly all the way home before I went back. I didn't think it would do any harm to just ask at the desk to make sure he had left. Maybe find out an address so I could bring him something at home. When the nurse told me Moses was still there in his room, I felt myself go numb.

Upstairs, I was even more surprised to find him, not sitting, but lying down. The TV was on, but Moses watched the ceiling. His face was drawn and tired, and he spoke in a soft wheeze.

"Are you okay, Moses?"

He closed his eyes and nodded. His cheeks had sunk in and lost color, and he seemed to have aged ten years in two days.

"I saw the truck today, Moses. The mechanic told me they pounded out that big dent in the side in ten minutes. All they gotta do now is straighten the frame a little. She'll be back on the road in two or three days."

The room was heavy with the smell of fading flowers. I hadn't really noticed before how many flowers people had brought.

"Yeah, I know all about the truck," he said finally. "Hank Gordon was in this morning to see me." Moses's eyes stayed trained on the ceiling.

I waited for him to continue, but he didn't. "Oh," I said blandly. I realized that Moses wasn't working his hands. Instead, they lay on the bed like two old gloves, eaten by rheumatism for fifty winters.

The voice finally continued. "Hank said I should vacation it for the rest of the winter. When I come back in the spring, they'll make me a platform boss."

His voice was as withered and thin as his hands, and I listened to the life oozing out through the cracks.

"Yes, but Moses," I whispered, starting to panic. "When are you going home? Did they tell you that yet? Damn, it's time to know, isn't it?"

The nurse came in, holding her finger to her lips, and led me out of the room. Moses just lay there, still watching the ceiling. I couldn't make myself tell him goodbye.

Piano Skirmish

Pudgy Thelma O'Day sat erectly in the old chair by the bay window as the afternoon sun slid down the pale yellow wall of the house next door, dimming to evening. Her hands gripped the padded arms, her feet were planted squarely on the floor, as if she were braced, six months ahead of time, for the onset of a blizzard. The veil of her squat brown hat was pulled down over her face, and she glared through it at Blanche LeMay, who sat with her legs stretched out in front of her on the far side of the room. Blanche was thin and pallid and white-haired. She feigned heavy-eyed disinterest, although her mind ran like a crabmeat picker as it sorted her thoughts. She held one elbow in her hand, her chin rested on her knuckles, and her forefinger extended back along her jawbone to her ear lobe. She hoped that her slow blink made Thelma nervous.

"In any event," Thelma said, "enough of the small talk. As you probably guessed already, I'm here about the piano. You said you'd decide this week when I could have it. You might just as well decide *early* in the week rather than later."

The piano in question was an old white-painted spinet that sat unimposingly in the corner of the room. Although Blanche had never played it, she did have it tuned every year.

"I said you could *have* it...?" Blanche asked absently.

"You said you'd *decide* this week."

"Oh. Then perhaps I'll decide *next* week."

Thelma stamped her foot. Her shoes squeezed her feet like two round wads of cheese, but she continued to like those shoes, as she'd liked them for almost twenty years, whether her feet had outgrown them or not.

"We've been talking about this for a year, Blanche. And the last month or so I've been trying to remind you almost every day."

"Yes," Blanche said dryly. "I'd noticed."

"Well, you keep putting it off. The doctors say Stanley will be out of the hospital next week, and I'd like to have that piano there for him when he gets home. You know how he loves a piano. And they say he may not be able to go back to work for six or eight months. A piano would give him something to do with himself." Blanche sighed. Stanley O'Day was not one of her favorite people, and the idea of such a wife-beating drunk ending up with her piano made her wince inwardly. But then again, hadn't the piano once belonged to Stanley? Blanche wasn't quite certain....

"It's not really mine to give away," she said finally.

Thelma leaned forward. "Then whose is it?"

"Cynthia's. When I die." Blanche let her lids sink over her eyes, as if to signal the end of the discussion.

Thelma leaned a few more inches forward. "That's right. And since you know that Cynthia has owed me a hundred dollars for over a year now—since she moved out of my house and left it such a wreck—that you might as well take and give that piano to me."

"Cynthia can take care of her own debts."

Thelma stamped again. "You've paid debts for every one of your children and grandchildren, Cynthia included. But just because I'm your best friend, you figure I have nothing coming to me."

"If Cynthia owes you money, collect from Cynthia. This isn't a garage sale. And it isn't a charity either."

Thelma lurched even further forward in her seat. "Charity! All I have is what little I make working. You have social security plus that fat pension Howard left you."

Blanche opened her eyes, stood up haltingly, then drew herself to her full height, which had been considerable in her younger years. "I'll have to ask you to leave now. I won't have Howard's name brought into this."

"Ask all you want. I'm staying right here until you give me that piano."

Blanche knew Thelma's demand was quite possibly reasonable, except that they had always owed each other something, and Blanche had lost track of whose turn it was to pay. Years ago she had decided that it was Thelma's, although she'd never been able to remember exactly what was owed to her or why. She suspected it had something to do with that ghastly Stanley—bailing him out of jail, perhaps. Or the time he borrowed Blanche's car and dented the fender.

Blanche teetered another moment, then started toward the kitchen. "Suit yourself. I'll just ignore you."

Blanche opened the refrigerator and took out one hard-boiled egg, one slice of bread, and a cellophane-wrapped saucer with four large strawberries on it. She set these items on the table but did not immediately sit down with them. Instead, she looked around the kitchen. She possessed many noises that Thelma detested, and Blanche proceeded to turn all of them on—the faucet that squealed, the fan with its bent propeller that grated every few turns, the old console radio that played only static. Once she'd activated all of them, Blanche sat down. She tried to ignore the noises, which she hated as much as Thelma did, telling herself that the price of victory had always been a certain degree of suffering.

Blanche ate slowly—even went back to the refrigerator for a fifth strawberry—but Thelma did not leave. Blanche looked up at the clock, yearning to watch her Tuesday television programs, but she refused to go into the livingroom. All around her, the kitchen belched and clanged and roared like a small but irate river. Blanche realized with growing annoyance that the racket was giving her a headache.

She took down the newspaper from the top of the refrigerator and searched for the crossword puzzle. She never worked crossword puzzles, and it took her fifteen minutes to find a word she knew. By that time her eyes began to cloud from the strain of trying to read without her glasses, which were in the now darkened living room. Ten more minutes passed before her curiosity drove Blanche to the living room doorway. As her eyes adjusted to the darkness, she saw that the chair Thelma had occupied was empty. Blanche started toward the end table where she'd last seen her glasses only to discover that Thelma had moved from the chair to the piano bench.

"I'm still waiting."

Blanche nearly lost her breath for a moment but said nothing. Her hands went about finding the glasses, then she fled again to the kitchen. She held onto the table for a moment until she calmed down, then she looked over her shoulder to see if the living room remained dark.

"I'd like to get home, Blanche," the voice came. "I haven't had my insulin shot yet today, and I don't feel very good."

Blanche hesitated, certain that she would seem stronger in silence, but the words leapt out. "Then go, damn you. You weren't invited in the first place."

Thelma's lumpy footsteps came into the kitchen. "You mean the piano is mine?"

"No."

"Then I'm going right back in that other room and sit there until it is."

"The piano is Cynthia's."

"That makes it automatically mine."

"You're making me angry now," Blanche quavered, looking straight at Thelma. "You're upsetting me."

"It's about time."

"If I have another heart attack," Blanche wheezed, "it will be your fault."

"Don't blame me for the way you used to overeat. And besides, don't forget who came to the hospital to see you *every single day* after your famous heart attack. It wasn't Cynthia. Or any of your other relatives."

"It's Cynthia's piano," Blanche glared.

"All right. Call her and tell her to come get it. Then I'll deal directly with her."

Blanche considered a moment. Cynthia had always claimed that the damage at Thelma's house occurred after she moved out, during the month the place was vacant.

Blanche believed her because she knew Cynthia to be an impeccable housekeeper.

Blanche lurched toward the telephone. "All right." She dialed slowly, trying to appear calm, but she knew Thelma was watching her trembling hand.

"Cynthia? This is your grandmother. I've decided to give you my piano. Tonight. When can you come over and pick it up? No, no, I'm perfectly all right except that I'm a little upset...no, just plagued by someone who's trying to burglarize my house. Will you come tonight? All right then, in the morning...no, Cynthia, this is important. Well, I don't care, I'm giving it to you anyway. I'll expect you in the morning."

"Huh," Thelma grunted. "She doesn't even want it, does she?"

Blanche was silent for a long time on the telephone. Thelma continued to mutter.

"Cynthia, come in the morning or don't come at all. Ever." Blanche hung the phone on the hook and went to the table where she sat down wearily. She didn't look at Thelma's gloating smile.

"I think one of my nephews can lend a hand," Thelma said. She picked up the phone and dialed quickly. "Hello, Chuck...it's me, Auntie Thelma...no, it's not very late, only nine...I need you to...well, I'm sorry if I interrupted you...listen, I'd like you to help move a piano. Blanche is giving Cynthia her piano and they need someone to come over in the morning and haul it to Cynthia's. Is the truck running all right?...good...I'll even have Blanche or Cynthia pass a couple of dollars along for your gas. About seven in the morning? Good. Thanks for helping your old Auntie. Good night."

Blanche stared at the squealing water faucet.

"You're going to have an awful water bill this month," Thelma said.

"I'm glad to see that old fan still works. Is that the one you got at the Salvation Army?"

Blanche continued to stare at the faucet.

"Oh well, if you won't talk, I guess I'll just go back in the other room and settle down for the night so that I don't miss Cynthia in the morning. Or Chuck."

Thelma hobbled into the dark living room. The moment she had disappeared, Blanche picked up the phone.

"Hello, Cynthia? I've changed my mind. I'm not giving you the piano after all, so don't come in the morning. No, I'm perfectly all right...no, never mind. Good night."

After she hung the phone up, she leaned her head into the living room. "You better call Chuck and tell him not to come."

"I won't let you be an Indian giver, Blanche. Poor Cynthia will be crushed if she doesn't get that piano. We'll bring it to her in the morning and let her decide when she wants to turn it over to me."

Blanche went back to the kitchen table. She tried to think, but her fantasies carried her from visions of having the police drag Thelma from the house to a flash of Thelma lying dead under the piano after Blanche had dropped it on her from a stepladder.

Thelma re-appeared in the doorway. Blanche could see that,

despite Thelma's smile, she was weary and quite possibly ill.

"I'm going to use your bathroom." Thelma slammed the bathroom door, and Blanche began to wish for some way to lock it from the outside.

If I were to become ill, she thought, Thelma would have to call Dr. Livingstone and explain what she'd done. And he, of course, would come immediately and demand that Thelma leave. It was her only hope, Blanche decided. Cynthia had just refused to come—or at least not offered to—and calling the police to have them remove Thelma seemed a bit much.

She heard Thelma flush the toilet and pulled herself out of her chair. The idea was preposterous, she knew, but she felt that Fate had presented her with no choice; she had to do whatever it took to make Thelma leave. Holding onto the table, Blanche lowered herself to her knees, then to all fours, then onto her side, and, eventually, her back. As a dramatic afterthought she kicked her chair over. It crashed to the floor, nearly on top of her.

In moments the bathroom door opened, and Thelma's heavy footsteps hurried to the kitchen. Blanche's head lay turned away, and she made no attempt to see the expression on Thelma's face. As the moments passed, Blanche became aware of how hard the floor was. She tried to remember the last time she'd lain on a floor, if ever.

"Blanche?"

Blanche began to wish that she'd dressed more warmly, or at least closed the kitchen window before taking to the floor.

"Blanche, I can see you breathing."

Yes, Blanche answered silently; the dying do breathe. The moments dragged on, and Blanche's skin-deep bones began to tingle. She wondered how long Thelma would wait and gawk before she called the doctor—if she called him at all.

"Blanche, get up off that floor before you hurt yourself. Do you want me to tell the whole town that you've lost your mind?"

Thelma sat down in the other kitchen chair, her breathing loud and labored. Blanche distracted herself from her own discomfort by listening to the rise and fall of Thelma's wheeze, which was barely audible above the sink faucet, the fan and the radio. But Blanche's mind soon came back to the pain in her neck and shoulder blades and elbows and spine. She tried once more to recall what it was that Thelma owed her. Was it the loan for a new furnace when Hiram took sick? Thelma would have had to sell the timber on her small lot to pay for the furnace. But Thelma had long ago repaid that loan. And hadn't Thelma also watered Blanche's plants every time she and Howard went away on vacation after Howard bought them that camper?

When Thelma spoke again, her voice was nearly a gasp. "What would Howard think if he saw this, Blanche? Do you think he'd be glad he left you that pension?"

After another few minutes of silence, Thelma got up and shut off the sound effects, beginning with the radio, then the fan, then the faucet. Blanche opened her eyes a slit as silence descended upon the room.

Thelma stood over Blanche and glared for a while, then went back to her chair. "Just a stubborn damn old Frenchman," Thelma muttered. "I don't know why I bother with you."

I'm not the Frenchman, Blanche wanted to say. That was Howard. *My* maiden name was *Hancock*.

"Oh, come *on*, Blanche. Get over it. That was forty years ago...."

Ah, so Thelma did feel some lingering sense of debt. Forty years ago? Blanche wrestled to place the years in order, all sixty-eight of them that she had known Thelma, starting when they were both being babysat all day by Blanche's great aunt, Tina, whose nickname was Tiny. Tiny was the broadest woman Blanche had ever known and used to...

"Or was it thirty years ago...?" Thelma mused aloud.

It's a trick, Blanche thought. She's just trying to make me sit up and ask her what in God's name she's talking about. What, that time Hiram kissed her in the kitchen? It was New Year's, for God's sake....

"I've forgiven *you*, if that makes a difference," Blanche said weakly. "I always had a mind that you'd done the same for what I did with Howard...."

Now Blanche had to pay attention not to breathe too hard or think too curiously. She tried to carry herself away to afternoons of picking blueberries or hanging out laundry in the days before Howard made enough at the post office to buy her a dryer—that scent of breeze-dried sheets that she used to love.

"Blanche, I'm not joking, I feel real woozy, like dying-type sick. I've got to have my insulin. Give me that piano so I can go home."

Blanche thought Thelma's voice lacked conviction. More

minutes stumbled by, and Blanche tried to imagine herself on a soft, floating mattress instead of the unforgiving floor. Even facing away away from the table, Blanche could tell that Thelma had taken up the unfinished crossword puzzle. She wheezed and sighed and whispered some of the clues. Blanche counted all the places on her that ached, then counted the ones where she felt nothing at all.

"Blanche, I'm warning you now...unless you want to hear my death-bed confessions of all the things I've done...especially to you...behind your back...you'd better...give me that piano and let me go."

The wheezing is purely fake, Blanche decided. And if it wasn't, Thelma would go home any minute.

"All right, Blanche...if you insist on hearing the worst...but don't blame me that I told you all about Howard...and me...in the bushes at Wood's Pond, or...in the barn cellar at my mother's place...."

Blanche pictured each place that Thelma mentioned and, with horror, pictured Thelma and Howard together there.

"It went on for years and years," Thelma droned weakly. "Neither one of us could quit. He could get me to do *anything*...things I never would have dreamed...of...with anybody else...."

Blanche felt herself grow colder, and her hands and lips began to tremble. She was about to stand up, grab a kitchen knife and slice off Thelma's face when a well-padded thud landed Thelma on the floor. One more wheeze, and the body settled on the floor just behind Blanche.

*****

Blanche's heart fluttered, and her eyes slapped open. Thelma's breathing was no longer audible, and at one point Blanche thought that it had stopped completely. Her head swung automatically toward Thelma before she realized what she had done, but Thelma faced the other way.

She's faking, Blanche told herself.

On the wall above the table hung Blanche's old clock. It was nearly midnight. She wondered what Thelma's next move would be. In the stillness, Blanche listened to the occasional car passing outside and to the frogs in the distance. But her various trains of thought became shorter and shorter, and each one ended at a new point of discomfort in her back or neck or hips.

As her resolve began to waver, the telephone rang. Her eyes scanned Thelma for signs of a reaction. The phone rang and rang—twenty-seven times, Blanche counted. She could hear all three extensions, and the clamor seemed loud enough to wake the entire street. She thought she saw Thelma gradually shift herself into a more comfortable position, and in the new silence cast by the unringing phone, resolve flooded Blanche once again.

Now that she could see the clock, the minutes crawled by even more slowly, and Blanche tried to forget the time by compiling a list of all the people who might have been calling. She was certain it was either Cynthia or Cynthia's mother, Dot. But she managed to enlarge the list to include everyone she'd met in the last ten years. She remembered aunts and cousins in Massachusetts who might have wanted to talk to her.

A car pulled into the driveway. Blanche could tell from the sound of the engine and the squeal of the alternator who it was. Cynthia knocked, waited only a moment, then burst through the door. When she saw the two old women on the floor, she groaned, "Oh, Jesus," and went straight for the telephone.

"Can you send an ambulance? For two. At the home of Blanche LeMay. I dunno, could be a heart attack with one and a diabetic coma with the other."

After she hung up, Cynthia covered both women with afghans from Blanche's bed, then paced the kitchen as she waited for the ambulance. After a few minutes, Cynthia, as Thelma had earlier, discovered the unfinished crossword puzzle.

Blanche listened for an approaching siren, but the police cruiser and ambulance arrived only with silently flashing lights. She tried to listen to the conversation between Cynthia and the paramedics, but her mind wandered to near delirium from her fatigue. Then she was lifted onto a stretcher. She felt comforted to be tucked into the warm, padded ambulance, and as soon as she was alone, she opened her eyes and tried to sit up.

Her comfort lasted only a minute; they soon carried Thelma out and secured her stretcher next to Blanche's. Thelma's breathing was audible again—the same rusty wheeze as when she first fell to the floor.

The hospital was less than a mile away. Blanche wondered if Thelma might really be ill and decided that even if she was, her diabetic coma was nothing compared to the heart attack that Blanche *might* have had. And that Thelma had made no gesture of concern, no attempt to call a doctor, and, instead, had only said all those ugly things—lies, every word of it, Blanche was sure.

They carried Blanche in first. Dr. Livingstone was already waiting for her in the emergency room, but she made no sign of recognition until they were alone.

"Ohhh, oh...." She opened her eyes.

The doctor bent over her with his stethoscope. Blanche smiled weakly and tried to sit up. He placed his hand against her shoulder to hold her down.

"Take it easy, Mrs. LeMay."

"I'm feeling much better," she said.

"You'd better just lie back here and rest," he said. "We almost lost you."

"Really? Well, I'm much better now. I think I can make it home."

"You won't be going anywhere for a few days. We need to run some tests."

"But I'm perfectly fine. I need to get home to protect my piano."

The doctor's expression grew more serious. They looked at each other for a few moments. Blanche had known him long enough to know when he was angry, as when she neglected to take her medication. She was a noncompliant patient, he'd told her on more than one visit. Now the doctor's jaw muscles tensed as she sat up and swung her legs around to stand up. She patted his shoulder.

"Really, Doctor.... I had a bit of a spell, but now I'm fine. Believe me."

Cynthia was in the lobby reading a magazine when Blanche came out. She pretended that she was still weak and let Cynthia help her out to the car. Cynthia opened the door for Blanche, then went around to her own side.

"Did they keep Thelma?" Blanche asked.

Cynthia looked at Blanche with a gleaning of comprehension. "As a matter of fact, she left just before you came out."

"She upsets me sometimes. Trying to get my piano...."

"Damn it, Grandma, she's been after that thing long enough, hasn't she?"

Cynthia started the car and put it in gear. As it lurched forward, Blanche swayed gently. She was sore all over and figured

she would be for a few days, but she also felt full of energy—
more so than she had in years.

"I think you ought to just give it to her, Grandma. She'll
keep after you until you end up just giving it to her."

Blanche pursed her lips a little tighter. "No...I don't think
so."

Cynthia's foot hesitated on the gas pedal, then surged with
sudden energy. She drove quickly along the carless streets. And
when Blanche was once again alone in her house with the windows closed and the air-tight, sound-tight house sealed off for
the night, she lifted the lid from the piano's keyboard, sat down
on the bench, raised both hands above the keys, and pounded
out a cacophony of meaningless notes until she could laugh no
longer.

In Search of Number Seven

Walter listened to the flight announcements as he sipped his second bourbon. Behind the bar, Manuel, the bartender, leaned against a cabinet, one leg crossed over the other, his elbows squeezing his copious middle as he wrote on the palm of his hand. His lips moved as he jotted, and Walter watched his thick, black eyebrows arch and settle, arch and settle. The lounge was dark and deserted, but just outside the open door people hurried by in intermittent herds.

"So what's so great about this Number Seven place?" Walter asked. "I heard you and that waitress who was here a few minutes ago raving about it."

Manuel shrugged and spoke without looking up. "It's the best lounge here in the airport, that's all."

"But what's so great about it? What makes it the best?"

"They leave you alone," Manuel said.

Walter gestured around the empty lounge. "I don't see anyone in your hair right now. How is Number Seven different?"

When Manuel looked up, his expression was hostile for a moment. He didn't like being doubted, Walter could see. Or even questioned.

"Everything's different. The people. The channels on the TV. The food."

Food, Walter thought. He hadn't eaten since breakfast. The hell with it. They'd serve dinner on the plane. A dinner flight home, after the four-day convention his bank back home in Manchester had sent him to. The one annual convention was his only travel since he'd left the Trust Department. During his eight years in Trust, he'd traveled all over the country. He used to go to the bars then. He'd made it a point never to call the waitress Sweetheart, or Sugar. He loathed men who did that. Walter's

approach was to go to an empty bar where the bartender was a
woman. If there were no other customers, the barmaid would
talk. After a while he would ask her out. He'd make up something about himself—he was an author, or film producer. The
women would inevitably refuse, and Walter would leave the bar
at what seemed a polite but unhurried time thereafter and go
back to his room, having left one of his fake business cards on
the table.

Now when he went to the conventions, he didn't go to the
bars. He bought a bottle and drank in his room while he watched
TV and dozed. In Miami Beach, though, he'd gone for a swim in
the hotel pool. It was adjacent to the lounge. He couldn't imagine coming to Miami Beach in January and not having a swim.
He wouldn't have to tell anyone that he'd only swum in the hotel
pool and only when it was empty, since he was too embarrassed
to let anyone see his thin, white legs and jiggling midriff.

"You ready for another, Amigo?" Manuel held the bottle toward Walter, who considered a moment, then shook his head
no.

"Peanuts?"

"No thanks." I'm his only customer and he's trying to hustle
a tip, Walter thought sadly. Maybe Number Seven has customers....

"You got a family, Manuel?"

"Me? Kids?" He laughed. "Hell no."

Walter laughed too. "That's the right idea. You look too
young to get tied down with a family."

"Me? I'm thirty-four."

Walter blinked. "Well, you look a lot younger. I thought you
were maybe twenty-five, twenty-six."

"Me? Hell no. I got gray hairs already."

"Say, what happened to your waitress, she desert you?"

"That girl was here? No, she works down in Number Two.
Me and her used to work together up in Number Seven. Before
they split us up."

Walter nodded understandingly. "I know what you mean. Say,
why don't you give me a tab. I guess it's that time...."

Manuel touched the icons on his computer screen, and the
machine drizzled out a slip of paper, which Manuel pushed across
the bar. Walter slapped his credit card on it.

"Add it to my budget deficit," he said. "We'll pretend I'm

Congress." He waited for Manuel to laugh or say something, but Manuel did not react in any way. If this guy's got a personality, my mother's the Pope, Walter mused as he left what he considered a minimal tip—one dollar on a ten-dollar and seventy-cent tab.

Out in the lobby, he checked his ticket again. Miami to Boston to Manchester. Back to cold, cold Manchester. He asked the first person he saw for the time. Another forty minutes, he gauged. He decided he had time for one more drink before getting on the plane. He would have it in the famous Number Seven. A quick one, just to see what the place was like.

As he rose to level two on the escalator, he remembered something Manuel had said about Number Seven being brighter. The first bar Walter came to was considerably lighter and had large, leafy plants growing in tubs. He looked for an identifying number above the entrance, but all the lounges in the airport had only a small, plain sign that said *Cocktails*. A half-dozen people sat at tables, and nearly that many sat at the bar. Walter opened the door and stood just inside looking around.

"What'll it be?" the bartender asked. He was young, blond, friendly. Walter found him a pleasant contrast to Manuel.

"Bourbon. On the rocks." Walter smiled back.

"Coming right up, Sir."

Walter's eyes wandered around the room. Nice clothes on the customers meant they had better jobs—at least with guys his age. Not with the young ones; their dads always bought them spiffy outfits for the interviews after school, then the kids wore their interview suits for the first couple of years on the job. Guys his age though, if they dressed well, were making it. Walter had to moonlight as an income tax consultant in season. He called it "taking in taxes, like taking in laundry."

Phyllis, his wife, had gone to work seven years before, and for a year or two they seemed to have enough each month to pay all the bills and even save some. But David's wreck in that car he and his buddies stole last September had erased eight years of savings, after the insurance company had refused to pay for David's hospital bills, since he was drunk. The whole carload of the little bastards were drunk, but only David's insurance coverage was voided, since he was the driver....

"Here's your bourbon on the rocks."

"Oh...yeah...thanks."

"Is this your first time in Miami, Sir?"

"Yes it is."

"I hope you're enjoying yourself. This is certainly the right time of year to be here. You're from the North, aren't you?"

"New Hampshire."

"Beautiful country. I remember going there once when I was a kid."

Walter took a big gulp from his drink. It was a bigger drink than he'd gotten in Number Three.

"Say, I believe I've witnessed a minor myth come true. This Number Seven is quite a place. I love all the plants and everything."

The bartender laughed. "This isn't Number Seven, it's Number Eight. But thanks just the same."

Walter set his drink on the bar. "Oh."

"Are you all right, Sir?" the bartender asked.

"Yes, yes...I do need to check the time, though."

"It's exactly five to six."

"Thanks. Gotta keep that in mind. Say, just where is Number Seven, anyway?"

"Right down the concourse here, Sir. I'd say it's about two hundred yards."

The waitress stood at the far end of the counter waiting to place an order, and the bartender hurried toward her.

Number Seven was probably like this, Walter thought. He began to wish that he'd come up here to wait for the plane rather than sitting in Number Three listening to Manuel complain for an hour. Maybe Number Seven was even nicer than this. Walter looked around again at the white stucco walls and stained glass windows and planters overflowing with vines. A large potted orange tree bowed with flowers and fruit.... That glass roof, it's like a damned greenhouse in here. Smell those miniature roses. Walter decided he had never been in a nicer bar. Why the hell didn't they have something like this in Manchester? He burned with a curiosity such as he had not known since he was in high school. He *had* to see Number Seven, just to see if it was anything like this place. Just to know where it was, in case the convention ever came to Miami again.

He took out his credit card and waited for the bartender, who was nowhere in sight. Why the hell don't I have five dollars in cash to leave for this guy so I can get myself out of here and catch that plane? All I have to my name is a twenty-dollar bill....

He glanced at his glass, which was still half full. The waitress was somewhere among the tables, her back to him. Walter realized he was only a few steps from the door. He could just leave, he thought. Slip out the door and get a glimpse of Number Seven, then run for the plane. He gulped the drink down and backed out into the concourse, closing the door quickly behind him.

A metallic voice echoed from the walls and ceiling announced the boarding call for Eastern flight two-two-two to Washington and Boston.

It wouldn't take but a minute, Walter told himself. He'd have his glance at Number Seven *and* get down to the gate on time, too.

He tried to run along the deserted corridor, but his heavy briefcase flopped against his leg, and his breath came fast and hard. He had to slow to a walk. His pulse beat in his throat, and his ankle began to hurt.

Walter heard running footsteps behind him. And voices.

"There he is, down there. Hey, you!"

Walter turned and saw two policemen running toward him. The blond bartender stood far down the corridor. Walter stopped, wavering on his feet. The alcohol caught him at about the same time as the police, and he collapsed for a moment in their arms.

"I'm all right, I'm all right," he kept saying.

His head hung as they walked him. Jailed in Miami. Wait'll the bank finds out.

The bartender wasn't angry. He even apologized.

"Sorry, Sir, I just needed to collect my money. The officers happened to be in the kitchen drinking coffee when..."

"Well I *wanted* to pay you. The PA said my plane was leaving, and you were nowhere to be seen."

"Sorry, Sir...when Nature calls..." He shrugged.

Walter laughed with relief as he handed over his credit card. "Well let me pay you and get out of here before I have to spend the damned night."

*****

Holding the briefcase under his arm, he was able to trot for a few seconds without the painful flopping. He felt mildly sobered by the incident and very fortunate, so when he came up behind the two policemen who had stopped him, he waved as he passed them. He pictured how they must have smirked at each other as he lumbered by.

At the entrance to the concourse, he had to wait while his briefcase was inspected.

"Hurry, please," he said.

Weary but still running, he saw his gate number just ahead. He thought about the bank and the thousands of pounds of paper he'd carried for them over the years. He'd never once carried his briefcase home empty. Other guys in the Trust Department had always laughed at him for toting home every brochure and pamphlet on display in the trade show exhibits. But it was Walter who had gotten the promotions, not them.

Madigan, who was supposed to have been a rising star until he made a fool of himself at a Christmas party, liked to call Walter a *pallbearer*. Walter had overheard Madigan describe him that way once. *He's a damned pallbearer. He shows up every time someone in this division gets canned. He got himself safely transferred to Securities and left us to fry. First one overboard when the going got rough. And now he comes over here to hustle the casualties off to the nearest bar whenever the hatchet falls.*

After he'd heard Madigan call him a pallbearer, Walter stopped going to the Trust Department altogether. Even after Ed Michaels, the last of the guys Walter had hired, got the axe.

Pallbearer.

He could probably get Madigan fired, Walter thought. Madigan had been transferred to Trust to be fired eventually, anyway. To be assigned to the Trust Division, even at a high salary, was the kiss of death at Granite National. Walter made a note to himself to get Madigan fired next week. And then show up and offer to take him out for a drink. See who thought he was so great then, the pallbearer or the corpse.

At the end of the corridor was the gate. The waiting-area was already empty. Walter started to run again, a labored, floppy wobble of a run that made his hip ache. When the ticket agent looked up and saw Walter, he signaled to Walter to slow down. Walter limped the last few steps to the desk and dropped his briefcase to the floor.

"How much did I miss it by?" Walter asked.

The agent grimaced. "I'd say about one minute. If you'd kept running, you could have missed it by only forty-five seconds."

Walter moaned and headed back down the concourse all the way to the ticket counters. An agent poked buttons on a computer as he mashed his lips back and forth against each other. Watching him made Walter mash his own lips.

"Miami to Boston...booked solid. I can put you on a flight that would take you to Chicago, then to Cleveland, Pittsburgh and Boston."

"Will I make my connection for Manchester?"

The agent glanced at the ticket, then at the computer screen. "No."

"Shit," Walter whispered. "All right. Just get me to Boston. My wife will have to drive down there to pick me up."

"I can get you out of here at midnight, guaranteed, but the best I can do before then is standby. Both of the evening flights are booked solid, and I've got a dozen or more already on standby."

Phyllis would raise hell, Walter thought. She loathed driving at night. He'd take a bus if she refused to pick him up.

"Book me on that midnight flight and put me on standby for the other two."

The agent told him that he'd buzz Boston and tell them to just hold his luggage.

Walter walked away smiling. He liked that. He'd buzz Boston one of these days, too. In the meantime, he'd buzz Manchester.

Walter turned away from the counter and began the long hike past the x-ray security machines, the escalators, Number Eight. Where did it say Number Eight?

He remembered that he needed to find a phone.

"I'll make a collect call, please," he told the operator. His quarter and dime rattled down into the coin return. Walter fidgeted as the phone rang and rang at the other end.

"Hello, Phyllis?"

"Oh God. I'm glad you finally called. Cheryl has run away from home."

"When? Where...?"

"I found the note this morning. I called the hotel you *said* you were staying at, but they said they didn't have any record of you."

"Our hotel got changed. Mine did, anyway. New secretary didn't make a guaranteed reservation for me. Plane was late getting into Miami."

"Walter, are you sure?"

"Yes, yes. Listen did she say where she was going?"

"Jamaica."

"Jamaica. They don't have any political troubles there I've heard about."

Phyllis began to cry. "I don't know...."

"No.... I don't think so. Stable place. Did she go alone?"

"No, that's the worst part. She went with Curtis."

"Oh. Well, he's a nice kid."

"Walter! How can you say that?"

"I like Curtis all right. I thought you did, too."

Phyllis said nothing for a moment. Walter listened to her sobs, which grew quieter.

"I ought to just hang up on you, Walter. Saying something like that."

Walter smiled. He'd begun to like the Jamaica idea—the freedom, the enormous world out there for a young person to see. Why the hell hadn't he just taken off for Jamaica when he was her age? Oh no, he'd gotten married and let himself become ossified in a boring job instead....

"Are you still there, Walter?"

"Yeah."

"Is it warm down there?"

"It's okay."

"What are we going to do?"

"Hell, it sounds like fun to me. At least she isn't alone. That would be bad if she was alone."

"Walter, she's traveling with a man and they aren't married."

"Hey...it's nineteen-ninety. They're having an adventure, for crying out loud? She's old enough to vote, she's old enough to screw. This day and age they all do, you know."

Another long silence. "I think you're disgraceful. What am I supposed to say when people ask me where she is?"

"Tell them she's gone to Jamaica."

"With a boy?"

"Just say she's gone to Jamaica. With a friend from college." Walter pictured Cheryl running on some Caribbean beach with Curtis. They'd been going together for six or seven months— fooling around for at least half that time, Walter figured. He could imagine them on some white-sanded beach with the setting sun on their tanned, nearly naked bodies.

"I suppose you'll also think it's an adventure when Cheryl

comes home pregnant?"

"She's too smart."

"It happens to the best of us," Phyllis said dryly.

Walter laughed. Nobody ever accused you of being smart, he wanted to say. But he didn't. "She asked me about that one time a couple of years ago. After she read a copy of her birth certificate. She said, 'If I was two months premature, how come I weighed almost nine pounds?' I told her she wasn't premature."

"You didn't!"

"If she was old enough to figure it out, I figured she had a right to know."

Phyllis began to cry again. "She must think I'm a common slut...."

"Actually, I think your stock rose a bit."

He heard a click.

Walter stared at the phone. She'd actually hung up on him. It was the first time he could recall that she'd ever done that. He laughed aloud, then replaced the receiver and started walking again. He never did get a chance to tell her he'd missed his plane, he realized.

He wondered how long he was going to have to wait before he'd find out whether or not he was going to get a seat on the seven o'clock plane.

What the hell, he thought. Just be glad you're not at home with her.

*****

There was undoubtedly time for another drink. He remembered that he never did get to see Number Seven. Was it worth the trouble? He was sure it would be just like Number Eight. Both on the same floor. He had the time, he still had the simmering curiosity. Plus, he'd be able to get something to eat, since he'd missed his dinner flight. Walter found Number Eight, then started down the concourse in what he assumed to be the direction of Number Seven. The passageways were filled now with deplaning passengers, and he wove his way among them. Air travelers looked generally happier than pedestrians or motorists, Walter thought. He guessed it was because the first reaction of most people upon getting off a plane was to be happy they were still alive. When he was younger and flying still made him nervous, Walter used to get drunk during his flights. Then, as he deplaned, he'd thank the pilots for saving his life. The pilots and flight attendants never seemed amused. Walter looked at the faces of individual passengers in the crowd and wondered if any of them had thanked the pilots—or felt an inclination to.

The police would never have caught him if the area had been this crowded, he judged. He would have gotten his glimpse of Number Seven, then gotten back to the gate in plenty of time.

But now he was glad he'd missed the plane. It was the weekend, he wasn't going to miss some early morning appointment, so why worry? His daughter was in Jamaica on spring break with a pleasant, intelligent, ambitious young man. His son had agreed finally to go to a private school instead of the public high school, where all his juvenile delinquent friends went. And his wife was finally dealing with an ancient denial. Wasn't life grand?

Walter came to the end of the corridor and still hadn't found Number Seven, so he retraced his steps. When he looked inside Number Eight, the young blond bartender waved to him. Walter hesitated a moment, then stepped inside.

"Miss your plane?" the bartender asked, looking concerned.

"Yeah. Hey, don't look so upset. You didn't know I had a plane to catch, and you couldn't very well call those two cops off after you'd already sicced them on me."

"But, I didn't mean..."

"Forget it. Why don't you pour me a bourbon while we're just standing here?"

The bartender came back with two glasses of ice and whiskey. "Happy Hour, two for one," he said. "And they're on me."

Walter laughed. "You don't have to do that...."

"I want to. That must have been terribly embarrassing, having the police chasing you down like a common criminal."

"Well, let's face it. At that moment I *was* a criminal."

The bartender shrugged. "You're being a little hard on yourself."

"Say, are you in school?" Walter asked.

"No. But I do just work here on weekends though. Second job."

"Oh? What's your other job?"

"I take people out deep-sea fishing."

Walter felt a small surge of admiration in his smile. "Hey, there's a career I could relate to."

"That's what everybody says."

Walter had finished one of the drinks and now started the

second.

"I book short cruises, too. My brother has a good-sized boat that runs out of Key West. They go island hopping on the weekend with small parties of ten or twelve people."

The bartender's smile grew large and inviting. "What are you planning for the weekend? Shoveling off your roof?"

"I don't believe you're doing this to me...."

He lifted Walter's empty whiskey glass and wiped the bar under it. "There's a flight to Key West in less than an hour. You could wake up on a yacht tomorrow morning...."

Walter crooked his neck to swallow the rest of his drink. "My daughter just ran off to Jamaica," Walter said, smiling at his empty glass.

"So can you, too...."

"You do all the booking?"

"Everything but the plane ticket to get to Key West. You do that yourself."

"And I can charge it all?"

"Every cracker crumb."

Walter fished through his wallet and brought out the credit card he thought probably had the most leeway.

"Sign me up."

*****

Walter went back down to the main lobby to buy his ticket for Key West. This is great, he thought. He looked at the wall posters that advertised all the places he could be going instead of home: the Virgin Islands, Venice, Jamaica. No, not Jamaica—he didn't want to crowd Cheryl. Let her have her adventure and he'd have his.

Ticket in hand, he went back upstairs to Number Eight. He sat at the bar and laid the ticket in front of him. When the bartender came over, glanced at the ticket and nodded approvingly.

"I made a call down to Key West while you were gone. Everything's all set."

"Wonderful. Just...wonderful. Say, what's your name?"

"Cal."

"It's a pleasure to meet you, Cal. My name's Walter."

They shook hands.

"Why don't you build me one last drink, now that we're close pals...?"

"That's not such a good idea," Cal said. "I don't want you to get too loaded. And you look kind of tired. Don't fall asleep."

"Wait just a damn minute...."

Cal's smile blushed out again. "I just want you to have a great time, Walter. Let me know how you like the cruise."

Walter's blip of anger was defused by the smile. They shook hands again. Cal leaned far over the bar and pointed.

"Right down there. Take the stairway down to ground level. It's a small airline. El Capitano. You can't miss it."

Walter immediately forgot the directions. As he continued down the corridor, he looked around for someone from whom he could ask more directions. He walked a long way, passing no one, but around the next corner, the El Capitano gate came into view at the far end of the concourse. Walter picked up his pace. The briefcase no longer seemed heavy, just unnecessary. Several people sat in the waiting area, and Walter looked from face to face. No one looked back. He noticed that the agent was watching him.

"Hey, is this the train to Heaven?"

The agent didn't seem amused. "Are you drunk, Sir?"

"I am like hell. I've only had two or three drinks."

"That doesn't make any difference. You're drunk."

"Well, you've got a hell of a nerve. I want to see the manager."

"There is no *manager*. This isn't a grocery store."

"Well then, I want to see the damned pilot."

"He doesn't want to see you."

"Well, by Jesus, I'll see him when I get on the plane."

"I'm afraid you won't be getting on the plane. There's a federal regulation that prohibits us from letting anyone who appears to be intoxicated on any plane. We stand by it, whether anyone else in the airline industry does or not."

"Well...*excuse me!*" Pious bitch, Walter thought. He was about to ask to speak to the president of El Capitano Airlines when the attendant looked at his ticket and shook her head.

"Have you been at Cal's bar?"

"Maybe I have, and maybe I haven't."

"Well, you're not getting on this flight. Do you want me to call upstairs and tell Cal to cancel your little *cruise*?"

Suddenly the whole idea struck Walter as ridiculous. He needed to get home. You never knew how stable any Caribbean country was, and David was supposed to be studying for a trigo-

nometry exam this weekend—one that would determine whether
or not he would graduate in June. And Phyllis might slip off the
wagon with her prescription drugs if he wasn't there to super-
vise....

The agent for his Boston flight reconfirmed his reservation.
That's the difference between the big airlines and the small ones,
Walter thought. The big ones don't hassle you over something
as petty as being mildly shit-faced.

"That flight will be boarding at about eleven-forty," the ticket
clerk said.

Walter glanced at the clock. A four-hour wait.

"Say, can you tell me how to get to lounge Number Seven?"

*****

Walter held firmly to the rubber railing of the escalator as it
pulled him once more toward the ceiling. His vision started to
sway, and he felt excited and exhausted.

Number Seven, he said to himself. He followed the directions the ticket agent had given him and walked on past Number
Eight with its plants and glass roof. Again the corridor looked
familiar to him, but he realized that it was because all the corri-
dors looked the same. He found himself suddenly by another
lounge, this one with a Roman numeral seven above the door.
He opened it and looked inside. He focused, finally, on the bartender who leaned against the counter watching him.

"This Number Seven?"

The bartender nodded, then looked back at his newspaper.
Walter looked around the empty lounge. This was the worst bar
yet, he thought. Dark, deserted, dingy. The bartender looked
almost like Manuel, and Walter wondered if maybe it was Manuel,
at last transferred back to Number Seven, as was his wish.

The bartender looked up at him again. "You want something?"

"Yeah, what time is it?"

"Seven forty-five."

"Say, do you mind if I take a little nap in here?"

"Go ahead. I don't care. You all right?"

"Just a little tired, that's all. Been a long week. I'll probably
get fired for some things I said to my bosses' best friends during
a convention. Most of my own friends have all been fired re-
cently. One of my kids lost a leg in an accident this year, and my
daughter just ran off with some young pimp."

The bartender shrugged, but said nothing.

"Can you wake me up in about three hours?" Walter asked.

The bartender looked back at his newspaper. "Sure."

Walter settled into a booth and let himself collapse against the wall. He stayed like that for a moment, then tried laying his head on his folded arms on the table. He felt much more comfortable that way, but he no longer felt sleepy. He picked up his head and looked at the bartender, who was definitely not Manuel.

"Say, can I ask you a question?"

"Sure." He didn't look up from his newspaper.

"You like working in Number Seven?"

"Naw. I used to work in Number Two. I'd rather be down there."

Walter laid his head back on his arms, and waited for his lids to slide over his eyes, which they did eventually.

Extreme Unction

Leland had not seen his pig, Cleopatra, in ten days. She had escaped twice before from her makeshift pen, but Leland had always found Cleo in the adjacent cornfield. This time, she'd made tracks in the mud, which had since frozen. The tracks led out to the orchard by the road. Leland figured that somebody driving by had seen the loose pig and just loaded her into their pickup and taken off.

Van appeared from the woods across the road. Leland could see that his neighbor had already been drinking. His face was ruddy, even in October, and his squat body seemed aged and weather-worn as he stood beside Leland, who was tall and lean. Both were in their thirties, although Van looked ten years older than Leland. Both men wore green John Deere caps.

"Well if it ain't Leland Phillip the Fifth," Van said.

"Shows what you got on your mind."

"What chew doing out here so early in the morning, Leland Phillip the Fifth?"

"Lookin' for my pig."

"Thought you already found her last week. What'd you do, lose her again?"

"No, she's still lost from the last time."

"Ain't that somethin'," Van muttered.

"What are you doing over in those woods—drinkin'?"

"Ay-uh."

"Where's Val think you are?"

"Out haying," Van said. "Which I fully intend to get to. Eventually."

Leland hunched his shoulders as the wind plunged at them, shaking loose the red and gold leaves and sending them swirling.

"Cold, huh?"

"Hell no," Van said, swaying slightly as he opened his jacket

47

to the wind. "Ts'warm out. Refreshin'."

"What you drinking?"

"Mogen Davis wine."

Van pulled the small bottle from his jacket pocket.

"Ugh. Got anything else?"

"Ay-uh. Whiskey."

"Well, you better get some hay in before you get too juiced."

Van nodded. "Fact is, I hay much better when I'm drunk than I do when I'm sober. I've tested it out."

"Where'd you get all the booze?"

"Studded my dog," Van said.

"Whaaat? Who the hell would pay for the services of that mutt?"

"Fact is, Max happens to be very good at that sort of thing."

"Get out of here...."

"They just wanted a big dog. Some folks from New Jersey. They campin' down by the lake and they had this Great Dane bitch that was in heat. There they was, stuck in a campground with two, three hundred other people camping there, too, and they had to clear all their stuff out of that Dodge van they was sleepin' in and store the dog in there 'fore she tore down the tree they had her tied to. Anyway, this guy pulled in. Had the dog in back there, you know, and he said he seen the sign for fresh eggs out front and he wanted a dozen. I could hear the dog in back there thrashin' around. Yowlin'. Well, just about then, old Max comes trottin' out of the barn. He smelled that bitch, you know, and this guy says, '*Damn*, that's the biggest dog I ever laid eyes on.' And Max stood right up and put his front paws up on the side of that van and stuck his head in the window sniffin' all around...."

Leland started walking. Van opened a pint of Wild Turkey and offered it.

"Want a bite?"

"Maybe just one little snort to keep from freezing to death."

Leland took a big swig and shuddered as it went down.

He got into his pickup truck, and Van got in with him. Leland put the truck in gear, and they bumped lethargically across the field.

"So anyway, this guy wanted to know what kind of dog Max was and I told him he was a Ethiopian retriever. Guy said he'd never heard of such a creature, but he sure as hell was big, and how much did I want for his services. Ten bucks, I says. He says, all right. So we brought Max around back of the van, the guy opened the door, and in went Max.

"Well, let me tell you—that was a sight to behold, that little camping van rockin' back and forth with them two dogs scrappin' away in there. We watched for a bit, then I went down back and did my afternoon milkin'. I told that fella if Val showed up and asked him who he was to tell her he was an insurance man. And don't be surprised if she pulls a gun before she gets to askin' who you are, I says to him.

"Well, I got the milkin' done and went up to see what was goin' on. Fella was asleep beside the van, and there warn't no noise coming from inside there with them two dogs, so I went back down to the barn and put a rebuilt generator on my truck, and when I come back he was settin' on the porch readin' a paperback book, and so I started fillin' in some ruts in the driveway. After a while he comes over and starts talkin'. Turns out he used to be a bartender down in New Jersey, and he quit that to become a travelin' booze salesman. I told him that sounded like a pretty good job, but he says it was awful 'cause he never got to see his family. Some people complain over the damnedest things, don't they? They ain't nothin' I'd like better than to see Val just twice a month or so.

"Anyway, I told him jokin' and all that anytime he had some free samples, to stop on by. And he says, 'You want some booze?' Next thing I know he lifts up his front seat and right there I see twelve, fifteen bottles. He says, Like scotch? I says sure. He hands me a fifth. Bourbon? Yep, I like that too, I says. Vodka? Sure. Regular American whiskey? You bet. Well, I stashed away six bottles before Val got back from the grocery shopping. Well, he wanted to see the cows, so I showed him the barn, and he says his kids might like to see the milkin' machines.

"Then he says, 'you think them dogs have had enough yet?' I told him I thought they was done quite a while ago. So, when we opened the door, Max come trottin' right out and took off around the barn. Julie was in there pantin' away, kind of half exhausted, half happy, and definitely calmer."

Leland grinned as he looked straight ahead.

Van gave him a light poke in the shoulder. "That story gettin' you horny, Leland?"

"No, but it's makin' me thirsty. Where's that jug?"

Van handed it to him. "Say, where are we headed?"

"Over to my place."

"What for?"

"Fella with all your booze oughta be kept in sight."

"What about my own work?"

"Hell, Van, you're just going to drink all day. Val can't bitch at you too much if you're over to my place."

"What about Theresa?"

"She said she don't feel good. Prob'ly stay in bed all day."

They pulled up in front of Leland's barn and got out. Van looked up at the sky. The wind had died down, and the clouds had turned from solid gray to patchy white.

"Might turn out to be a sunny day after all," Van sighed.

"'Bout time. Been like December for the last week."

They entered the barn where the air was dense and dry with dust. The straw on the floor had been crushed to a fine grain, which muffled their footsteps.

"We can sit on them bales over there," Leland said, pointing.

Van took out the bottle. "Yessir, I sure wouldn't mind bein' a booze salesman." He slugged from the bottle and passed it to Leland, continuing to stare as Leland tipped the bottle without letting it touch his lips. "Been a while since you took a day off to sit around and drink," Van said.

"You don't usually have anything fit to drink. 'Sides, the kids are off at school, Theresa's up there in bed. Weather's starting to warm up. Everything's just right today. Fact, it's a perfect day to get drunk."

*****

A frown came to Van's face as he slowly turned his head in one direction, then another. "You smell somethin' funny?" he asked, sniffing.

"What? No, I don't smell nothing. Had a stuffy nose since this cold spell set in."

"God..." Van's face contorted, and he pinched his nose shut. "What's it smell like?"

Van slid his jacket off and undid the top button of his shirt. "Smells like something's either dead or tryin' awful hard at it."

Leland tried to sniff, but his nose was hopelessly blocked. "Can't smell nothing."

"Well, you're lucky."

They stopped talking when they heard the rattle of a stiff,

second-story window being forced open.

"Lelaaaaaand!"

Leland got up and strode to the doorway. Theresa's dark, curly hair was ruffled, and Leland noticed the way she held her robe only slightly closed, leaving a gentle crease down her front.

"What in God's name is that smell?" she asked.

"What smell?"

"Don't tell me you can't smell that."

"I ain't smelled nothin' in two weeks."

"Well I can't stand it. It's giving me a headache."

"Here, I'll come in and take a look around the house. Maybe the dogs got into the garbage or something."

Leland went into the bathroom just off the kitchen, squeezed some toothpaste onto his finger and rubbed it against his teeth. Then he swished water around his mouth until he was satisfied that the smell of liquor was gone. He tossed his cap on the counter beside the sink and ran a brush through his hair as he watched himself in the mirror.

When he started up the stairs, the whiskey rushed to his head, and he began climbing two steps at a time. Theresa was back in bed with the pillow pulled over her head. He sat on the edge of the bed and set his hand near the form of her hip under the blanket.

"Hey, how you feeling?"

"Sick to my stomach. Can't you please do something about that smell?"

"Yeah, I think I did already. Just some garbage down by the cans...."

"This isn't a garbage smell."

"It's all taken care of anyway. Say, how would you like a little bit of..."

"That stink is too strong, Leland. I can't stand it."

Leland looked up at the open window. "Here, I'll take care of that smell right now."He forced the window down, then his eye caught a can of aerosol room deodorant on the bureau. He briefly sprayed the room then pulled the bedroom door shut.

"You can come on out now," he said.

Theresa pushed the pillow part way back and brushed the hair out of her eyes. "I'll bet it's that pig," she said. "Garbage just doesn't smell like that."

He sat back down on the edge of the bed. This time he let his hand touch her leg. "Feel any better?" he asked.

"Not really."

"Do you feel like a little...you-know-what?"

"Not with that smell out there."

"You can still smell that, huh?" He got up and reached for the spray can again.

"No, please! That plus the other..."

He edged back down onto the bed. "So I take it you're not in the mood?"

She pulled the pillow back over her head. "Get rid of that smell and we'll see."

Leland stood up almost too quickly.

*****

When he opened the bedroom door, the smell suddenly penetrated his clogged nostrils in a single blast, and he staggered a moment as he tried to catch his breath. Outside in the hot sun, the stench made his eyes water. He found Van in the barn where he had left him. Van held the bottle of whiskey directly under his nose and breathed through his mouth.

"We gotta do something about that smell," Leland said. "I guess it probably is my pig. My *former* pig, that is."

"You mean *you* gotta do something about it. I'm going home."

"Wait a minute. You can't just leave me like that. What about the time I helped you clean out your septic tank when it clogged up and overflowed? Wasn't exactly my idea of a picnic."

After a moment, Van screwed the cap on the bottle and struggled to his feet.

Leland looked at the bottle. "You better leave that here."

"I ain't goin' lookin' for no worm-eaten pig without a little something to brace up with." He tapped his bulging pockets. "In fact, I got two more like it right in this shirt."

Leland's eyes began to water again. "Let's start out back," he said.

Behind the house, the smell trailed off.

"I'll bet she's in that old privet patch in the front yard," Van said. "I'll lay you odds."

They started around to the front of the house, and the stench grew so thick that Leland almost thought he could see it. Van held his nose with one hand and the bottle with the other. The sun, which had grown hotter, burned down on their necks and shoulders. Leland's flannel shirt began to itch. As they neared the privet patch, the flies buzzed in panic for a few moments before settling back into the dense shrub.

"You're right," Leland said. "Let's get a saw and some shovels."

In the barn they each took another long slug. When they approached the thicket again, the flies seemed bolder, less inclined to flee; but then Leland began to saw at the spindly branches, and the flies rose like smoke from the privet. Van ducked and swatted and backed away from the bush. He took the bottles out of his shirt, took one more swig, and laid all three bottles on the ground.

Leland sawed furiously, ripping away the branches before the blade had gnawed all the way through. He noticed Van standing watching him.

"You dig while I saw," he said.

Van approached slowly, using the shovel to steady himself. "Dig where?"

"Right here in back of me."

"You're gonna bury that thing right here in the front lawn?"

"That's right. Unless *you* want to carry it out back yourself."

Before Van began to dig, he drenched his handkerchief in whiskey and tied it over his nose. He dug furiously at the soft ground, his eyes squinted tight and the handkerchief fluttering as he gasped and gagged. After a few minutes, he stopped and stood still, heaving as he gaped.

"This stinks so bad, I think it's making me sober."

Leland had sawn down half of the privet patch. "Just keep digging."

Van dug some more, although not as vigorously. In a few minutes, he'd dug a hole that was two feet deep. He set his foot on the blade of the shovel.

"I can't go on," Van said quietly. He slipped the handkerchief off his face to take a drink. He gulped once, then once again. When he tried to screw the cap on the bottle, he couldn't seem to make a connection. The sun broke through the last shreds of elm that had partially shaded them, and the jiggling shrub became a steaming haze through Van's bleary eyes. When he blinked, the sweat dribbled from his brows into his eyes.

"Leland..." he said weakly.

"Damn it, Van...get ahold of yourself."

Van looked past Leland to the privet patch and the now exposed pig. Van crumpled to his knees. One knee slipped over the edge of the hole he had been digging, and he flipped over onto his back with one hand raised.

"In the name of the Father and of the..."

"For God's sakes, some help you are!" Leland grasped Van's ankles and dragged him out of the hole.

Lying on his back, Van blessed the blue sky: "...and of the Holy Ghost...."

Leland grabbed the shovel that lay across Van's chest and began to dig with even more energy than he had vented on the sawing. In no time he was nearly waist-deep. He stopped to look around. Van was trying to get up.

"Jesus Christ, I can't stand that smell."

"Well then help me shovel instead of getting drunk and falling all over the place."

With that, Leland shoveled again, red-faced and streaked with dirt and sweat.

Van held the handkerchief over his face again, and now he stumbled to his feet and lurched toward the bottles.

"I can't stand that god-awful smell," he said, shaking his head, wide-eyed. He opened a new bottle and staggered toward the privet patch, eyes clamped shut, nostrils as collapsed as he could make them. Without looking down, he emptied the whisky bottle over the pig's carcass.

"Bless me Father, for I have sinned.... It's been twenty-two years since..."

"What in God's name are you doing now?"

"Deodorizing this pig."

"Here, help me get it into this hole."

Leland handed him a shovel. They climbed into the privet patch, straddling the wirelike branches, and pried their shovels under the carcass. After they had maneuvered the rotting pieces of the pig out of the privet, Van stumbled getting out himself, and instinctively fell away from the pig. Leland didn't notice, so intent was he on getting the pig buried. He half-rolled, half-shoveled his pig's remains into the hole and began to cover them. When the carcass was barely covered, Leland threw more dirt on the ground beside the hole and into the privet patch where the pig had lain for ten days.

When the shovel dropped from his hands, he did not bend to retrieve it. Instead, he bent to pick up the nearly depleted whiskey bottle and emptied the last swig into his parched throat.

Van had fallen down again and lay on the ground mumbling. "...and of the Son..."

Leland wavered a moment, then stumbled into the house, stopping to lean against the cupboard just inside the kitchen. Theresa came into the room with a scarf wrapped around her face. Leland thought he smelled Vick's Vaporub and was grateful for the new odor.

"God, you look half dead," she told him, glancing at the whiskey bottle in his hand. "Not somethin' a fella usually does sober," Leland said. He watched the hem of her robe flit about her calves as she cleared the breakfast dishes. He glanced at the clock. "Damn. Kids'll be home from school in a couple of hours."

She winked. "That's plenty of time." She looked at his hands and clothes.

"Yeah, I know.... I was just going up to take a bath."

"Maybe you should leave those clothes outside to air," she said, running water into the sink. When she glanced behind her a few moments later, the clothes were in a heap on the floor and Leland had disappeared. Moments later she heard the water running in the shower upstairs. She glanced out the window to where Van lay beside the mutilated thicket. And even though she figured he wouldn't be getting up for a while, she turned the key in the lock anyway.

Widening the Road

The first two mornings, Porter had held the fox in the sights of his rifle, waiting for the fox to make a move, but on the third morning, he watched through his binoculars as the fox sat calmly, nestled in the middle of the field like a stone in the clean, hard snow. The rifle stayed leaning against the dresser beside the window.

The fourth morning, the fox did not appear. Porter waited at the window from daybreak until Marion woke at seven to the alarm. He waited for her to ask him what he was doing but she didn't. Now it was the fifth morning and the fox was back. Porter knelt, watching the field, the cold air settling in the sleep-moist creases of his face. He expected the fox to sit still in the same place, as it had all week, then inexplicably bolt back into the woods. The bed stirred behind him.

"Porter...?"

He said nothing.

"Porter, what are you doing?"

"Nothing."

"Then maybe you could do it with the window shut?"

A moment passed, then she tossed herself back down on the bed. He glanced at the bundle she made against the dark wall. She always got cold easily, he thought, recalling once again how Marion's mother had warned him that the girl needed to fatten up—that she should eat three or four bananas every day to put on some weight before the wedding. Marion hadn't eaten bananas, though, nor much of anything else. She'd never been sick, either. Not since she'd had strep throat in the seventh grade. They'd begun to date in high school, then got married after Porter spent three years in the army. Marion's mother had insisted that he wear his uniform for the wedding. He agreed, since it meant he would not have to spend money renting a tuxedo. Mama Finch liked Porter's attitude toward money and assured him that Marion would be easy to support.

"She doesn't eat anything," Mama Finch had said.

"What does she like best?"

Mama Finch smiled as if she were announcing an increase in Marion's dowry. "Breakfast. The cheapest meal to fix at home, and the cheapest one to eat out."

Porter knew that already, although he pretended to Mama Finch that they had never eaten breakfast together. That seemed almost too much of a confession that they'd slept together the night before.

"Porter, what's out there?"

"Nothing. Just a fox."

Marion threw the covers off and padded to the window. "I don't hear the hens...."

"He wasn't close enough to get them going."

He felt her in back of him, although she didn't touch him. He watched her breath drift out the window after his own.

"Where?" she asked.

"He's gone."

"Where was he?"

"Over there. Near the stone wall."

"That wasn't where you were looking just now," she said.

"He moved."

"Are you sure?"

"You calling me crazy?"

She backed away from the window and he listened to her crawl into the bed.

"Is that gun going to sit there for another week?" she asked.

Porter didn't answer. He looked for the fox again, then lowered the window. He dressed quickly and went downstairs.

They owned an electric percolator, but Porter always made instant coffee. He poured himself a bowl of cold cereal. By the time he'd peeled an apple and sliced it onto his cereal, the water for his coffee was boiling.

Before he sat back down, he turned on the radio to listen to Country Joe-Eddie who played fiddle and sang with his three daughters between portions of the news and farm reports. Eggs were going up, grain was going down. That was nothing new, Porter thought. It was usually followed by a period of grain shortages and a glutted egg market, meaning feed would be up and eggs down. And he was having to sell his entire stock to the Portland middleman, now that the local merchants had begun their boycott against him.

Country Joe-Eddie was back.

"...Now I eat all alone at a table for two...and I never was lonely...until I met you...."

He heard Marion on the stairs. She wore a light blue parka over her bathrobe. Her hair was blond in the summer but nearly brown in the winter.

"I don't like that gun up there," she said.

"What's the matter with it?"

"It scares me." She started across the kitchen to the coffee pot. She refused to wear the slippers her mother bought her each Christmas and instead wore a pair of Porter's old basketball sneakers. He watched the untied laces flop as the soles slapped the cold linoleum floor. He hoped she would make herself some instant and take it back upstairs with her, but she used the percolator instead, washing it first with soap rather than just rinsing it out. After she'd dried it and set it up to percolate, she made herself a cup of instant and left the room. He listened to her thump back up the stairs. Then he listened to the percolator.

She was wise, Porter thought. She always got out of the room when she sensed he could get angry about something. He'd even thanked her for her good sense, once, before the problem over the road made it impossible for them to talk about anything.

"Don't you think I'm easy to live with just as long as nobody pisses me off?" he'd asked her. They'd been married about five months at the time. It was a Sunday morning when Porter had driven the five miles into Hampton to get fresh doughnuts at the bakery.

"Yes," she said as she stood at the sink in her short terrycloth robe cutting up strawberries. "And one of these days you may grow up. We should have some babies after you grow up," she added.

Porter had been dismayed as he realized for the first time in his life that maybe sometimes he was annoying.

When the percolator stopped, he poured himself a cup of coffee. He was ready for his breakfast cigarette, but when he patted his breast pocket, he remembered that the cigarettes were on the nightstand beside the bed. Upstairs he found Marion again knot-

ted into a bundle under the blankets. Her empty cup sat on the
nightstand. He stood near the bed a moment before he picked up
his cigarettes and started out of the room.

When he glanced into the field as he passed the window, the
fox was back, moving in quick, short leaps toward Porter's
chicken-coop. He grabbed the rifle before he remembered that
Marion had closed the window. By the time he was in position
at the window, the fox had again disappeared, and the hen house
came alive with a single screech, then another, then forty, then
four hundred. He kept what he assumed would be the fox's exit
in his sights, and when the fox came back into view dragging a
chicken, Porter squeezed the trigger.

The gunshot seemed like an explosion inside the house.
Marion screamed. He fired four more times before the fox
plunged into the woods, and Porter could only stare at the fox's
sudden absence.

When he looked back at Marion she had pulled the quilt over
her head. He hurried down the stairs and ran from the kitchen
out to the chicken coop, where he saw right away that the door
had been left ajar—his own fault, he remembered, for trying to
carry too many eggs at once and kicking the door shut rather
than stopping to fasten the latch properly. He noticed chicken
tracks in the snow just outside the door and shook his head over
how easy the hens had made the fox's job.

The hens were in an uproar, and their unanimous panic made
Porter want to turn the rifle on them for over-reacting. Every-
one, most of all Marion, was over-reacting. Only the fox and
Porter had played their roles reasonably.

He followed the fox's tracks a few yards A hit, he told himself. A definite hit. The farther Porter followed the tracks, the
more blood he saw. He ran back to the house. Marion was in the
kitchen.

"I hit it," he said, leaning the rifle in the corner by the door.

He glanced at her, but she said nothing. He opened the drawer
in the kitchen table and filled the pockets of his jacket with am-
munition, then stuffed some cookies sitting on a plate into his
shirt pockets.

"Where are you going?" she asked. The tinge of panic in her
voice made his breath come faster.

"Run down that fox! Where the hell do you *think* I'm going?"

"But I thought you killed him...."

"Hit him. Not killed him."

"He won't be back, will he? Not after you hit him?"

"I want to make sure."

She looked more at the gun than at him. "Are you sure you shouldn't work around here instead?"

He didn't answer. Questions like that infuriated him.

In the shed he found his snowshoes. The air settled around him, and the light wind tried to peel the skin from his face. He carried the snowshoes to the edge of the woods and sat on the trunk of a fallen tree to put them on, in sight of the fox's track. The blood in the fox's tracks was pink and distinct.

*****

Porter walked all morning. The fox stayed far enough ahead of him to remain out of sight, but Porter knew from the ragged tracks that he was gaining ground. He spent most of the time thinking. Only when the tracks changed direction did he pay attention to the pursuit. At one point he realized that the fox was traveling in and out of his property, and four times Porter climbed through the electrical barbed-wire fence that surrounded his land, knowing an alarm sounded in his cellar each time he touched the fence. Marion was ready to leave him, or so she claimed, over the installation of the fence. Porter had it put up when the disagreement over the new road construction had degenerated to a battle between himself and an alliance of the highway department and the Hampton Merchants' Association.

The state wanted to widen the road that went by his house. The Hampton Merchants' Association wanted the new road, too. The proposed construction would remove all the roadside trees on Porter's property—eight old maples and one of the few healthy elms in that part of the state. Half his lawn was to be a paved shoulder on the new four-lane. The government had offered him two thousand dollars for the trees and the property, but Porter rejected the offer and got a court order to halt construction of that portion of road that bordered his land. Assuming the matter would be settled quickly, the state highway department had begun construction of the new road, completing the stretch from town to Porter's farm and continuing past his place to the lake and beyond. But in front of Porter's property, the four lanes bottle-necked to a narrow, pot-holed two-lane that was bordered by Porter's electrical fence, which he had erected after someone threw the carcasses of ten slaughtered hens on his lawn.

Now the fence extended around his entire sixty acres, and whenever anything brushed against the fence, a buzzer sounded in his basement. Marion accused him of turning their home into a war zone. Porter said if war was what it took to protect your house, then war was what you did.

The state set up a public hearing. Porter suggested that they curve the highway away from his place, through the woods, so that he wouldn't have to see the road at all. The highway department representative stated that the whole purpose of rebuilding the road was to make it safer by eliminating the curves. Porter countered by saying that to the best of his knowledge, no one had ever been hurt or killed on that road, and if they really wanted to make it safer, they should leave the old road, lower the speed limit to twenty-five, and dig more potholes to make sure people drove slowly.

That would raise the cost of the new road considerably, the government man explained. Having to reroute an entire road that was nearly finished would cost millions. He also made a new offer to Porter, three thousand dollars, and asserted that this was double the actual value of the land.

"Don't make me laugh," Porter said. He glared at the government man's pocked face and hairy fingers. His suit, which seemed incongruous on such a burly, bearish slob, made Porter hate him, and the government man's tired, bored expression made Porter hate him even more.

"How much *will* you take, then?"

"Ten thousand," Porter said.

The government man, the Merchants' Association, and the judge who had issued the injunction against continuing construction of the road decided than an impasse had been reached. That was the last Porter had heard, almost two weeks ago, from the government. But a few days later, all the local food retailers refused to take his eggs.

"You like all those out-of-towners throwing beer cans on your lawn all summer long?" Porter had asked one storeowner.

"It don't cost nothing to pick 'em up," was the squint-eyed answer he got.

Porter hated the traffic in town in the summertime. Mostly station wagons, he'd noted. Most of them full of bratty kids. It wasn't just the beer and soda cans on his lawn that annoyed him.

In ten years he'd had six dogs and a dozen or more cats run over, always during the summer.

"Tie them up," one camper suggested when he stopped to buy eggs, and Porter happened to complain to him about losing a dog just the night before. The man wore a tee shirt that was too small—with letters that said, "Life's a bitch and so's my wife."

"I don't live out here in the country to tie my dogs up, mister. It's you summer people that think you can come up here and drive like you do down there in Boston."

The customer soured immediately. "Hey, what are you bellyaching about? You're making a buck off the summer people."

"Not enough to make it worth the aggravation."

The man stuffed his wallet back in his pocket. "Then I'll make sure we don't come back and aggravate you...."

"Good. I hope you take your vacation in Ohio next year!"

*****

Porter shifted his rifle to the other shoulder and stopped at the crest of a hill where he looked out over the sea of snow and, beyond that, the dark, colorless islands of pines. The fox's tracks had led back to the power-line trail that skirted his south pasture. He took off his glove and felt the fox's track with his finger. The two left tracks were distinct but the right paw marks were obliterated by the dragging of the hind leg. There was no longer blood in the tracks and Porter supposed the leg had probably frozen from lack of movement. He thought about his own feet and noticed that the left one had begun to feel numb. He worked it inside his boot as he glanced at the overcast sky that was slightly brighter where the sun lurked. Porter guessed it was early afternoon.

From the crest where he stood he could see the southbound portion of the new road and the flashing lights that warned motorists of the construction ahead. He smiled as he thought about how he had single-handedly brought a whole road to a tired wheeze, if not an outright halt. If they'd pay enough for me to build a new house way back in the woods on this land, I'd call it a deal today, Porter thought. But the ten thousand he was asking for wouldn't pay for the wood for a new chicken coop, let alone a house. And he knew the state would never pay him that much anyway.

Hiram Wainwright had stopped by the Sunday afternoon before and sat at Porter's kitchen table, alternately smiling and scowling as he spoke, which made Porter wonder if he'd rehearsed his repertory of expressions before the visit. Wainwright looked fat and judgmental in his dark, pin-striped church suit.

"People traveling through here get word that the road from Portland to Norway isn't finished yet, so they go around the Harrison side of the lake," Wainwright said. He had appointed himself spokesman for the merchants in town. "They could be coming through here and spending their money on gas and hotdogs and charcoal briquettes and eggs and all sorts of stuff. Hell, man, you've put up that fence...you could have a herd of cows and sell milk and ice cream and who knows what."

Wainwright cocked his head and raised his arms up from his sides whenever he thought he had brought common sense into a senseless conversation. Then he dropped his arms loudly as if he alone held the only common sense in the room. "Look, Porter, I don't like the summer people any better than you do, but I'll put up with them for three months of the year because then I can relax for the other nine."

Porter made it a point to remain silent, not get angry, not laugh, not taunt. Marion had begged him to just listen—listen and ask honest, non-antagonistic questions. They had no choice as far as she was concerned. Sooner or later the state was going to make them sell the land—and at whatever price they, not Porter, decided. Even if they got the outlandish amount Porter was asking, half of it would go to the lawyer in Norway that Porter had insisted on hiring.

Porter listened, and, after an hour, Wainwright left.

"All they have to do is put a bend in the road," Porter said after Wainwright had gone. Marion sighed, shook her head, and went to bed at five-thirty. Porter fell asleep watching a hockey game on TV.

He got up from the rock where he sat and continued down the power-line trail. It was too cold to sit in one place too long. He remembered films from army basic training that showed troops in the Korean War who had been frostbitten. He remembered the way their missing toes made them limp. He began to walk faster to generate some heat in his boots and almost walked by where the tracks cut into the woods that bordered the lake. Porter had planted Christmas trees in one section but then couldn't bear to harvest them; they just looked too right, growing there on the hillside.

In the woods it was much darker. The snow lay so thickly in the pine branches above that very little light got through, even on a bright day. It was warmer in the woods, and he undid his scarf and scratched his neck, wishing he'd brought more to eat— a banana or more of Marion's oatmeal cookies, which he'd eaten hours ago. Hearing the brook in the distance, Porter realized how thirsty he was. He came to his fence again and maneuvered between the wires. He wondered what Marion did each time the buzzer went off. She claimed that since the installation of the fence, people in town avoided her, and that some people thought Porter was having a nervous breakdown. Good, he'd told her— they'd be sure to stay away.

As it grew warmer, he unzipped his jacket. His hands felt sweaty in the fur-lined gloves, and he took them off and stuck them in his pocket. The scarf went into the other pocket.

The snow melting from the branches dripped onto the nearly snowless pine needle floor. What little snow had accumulated on the ground lay in soggy patches with rounded, sparkling edges. The clatter of the brook grew louder, and by the time he reached it, the sound had become a roar in the silent forest. The banks of the brook were thick with ice, but the water rattled freely among the snow-capped rocks. Kneeling on a rock near the edge, Porter scooped the icy water to his mouth, then sat against a tree. He smoked two cigarettes and decided there was no point in the chase, but that there was no point in going back to the house, either. The lake was just a little farther, and as he neared the end of the woods, he zipped up his jacket and put his gloves back on. After the darkness of the woods, the white mass of the lake made his eyes water. When he was able to focus again, he saw the fox crouched out on the ice, not twenty yards from him.

*****

At first Porter thought the fox was a mirage, especially when it did not try to run away, but then he remembered the fox's wounded leg.

"Hey there, big fella," he said.

The wind played in the fox's mane, making him puff out at moments, shrink at others. After a moment, the fox resumed licking its wounded leg.

"Sorry about that," Porter said. "Kinda looks like you've run out of steam."

Porter watched the fox and the fleeting funnels of wind that

swirled the snow up into tiny ghosts and twisted them away.
When he brought his eyes back to the fox, Porter raised his rifle
to his shoulder and held the fox in his sights.

The fox alternated between licking its leg and studying Porter. When Porter lowered the rifle to his side, the fox's mouth
drooped open and its tongue hung out.

"I'm listening, fox. I know you've been coming around all
these mornings to tell me something. Am I supposed to sell or
not?"

The fox's steamy panting stopped as it stared. Porter thought
it looked small and young, and he imagined the fox crippled for
life, having to depend on the other foxes for food and protec-
tion. It was no way for a fox to have to live.

"Sorry about that, but if it'd been me messing with your
chickens, you'd have done the same."

Porter remembered the way Marion had screamed when he
shot at the fox from the bedroom window. It seemed odd to him,
her uneasiness about the gun. She was not a hunter, but she always went with Porter when he hunted. She'd walk along in back
of him, sometimes so quietly that he'd turn around to make sure
she was still there. She carried a rifle, like him, but without am-
munition.

"You married, fox?" Porter smiled. "No? Just living together?
That's probably the best way."

The fox stood up, wobbled for a moment, then hopped two
steps away, nearly tripping on its stiff hind leg. When Porter
raised the rifle again, the fox bared its teeth and snarled.

"I don't blame you. I know it must hurt like hell. I could do
you a favor and blow your brains out. What do you think? Just
say the word, and I'll put you in that big henhouse in the sky."

He could hit the fox anywhere from this range, he thought.
Quicker death than any suffering creature could ask for. Once
more the fox wobbled to its feet and hopped a few steps. Porter
lowered the rifle.

"All right. There's an answer. Don't shoot. You'll get over
the damaged leg and survive, right? Just like I should hold out
on the land and make them curve the road away from the house."
The fox slowly picked its way among the isolated drifts of snow,
and after a minute of watching its pained moves, Porter walked
back into the woods. Any fox who can go as far as he has with a
wound that bad has what it takes, he thought.

By the time he got home it was nearly dusk. The lights were on in the kitchen, and the coffee pot was still plugged in. He unplugged it, dumped out the tarlike residue and started a fresh pot. When he sat down at the table, he found her note.

Dear Porter,

I've decided to let you stay by yourself until this whole thing about the road is over and you get back to normal. Everyone is worried about you, myself included. I waited for you until two o'clock, but I guess chasing the fox was more important than feeding the hens. I wanted to talk to you one last time before I did this, but I just couldn't wait any longer. Call me at my mother's if you have anything you want to say. Sorry this had to happen, but I can't take the fences and the alarms and the guns and your mood swings anymore.

Love always,

Marion

Porter threw the letter on the floor. He thought about calling her to tell her that she'd been more trouble than she was worth these past seven years. Instead, he went out to feed the hens. The fox had unsettled them that morning, so there weren't many eggs for him to collect.

He finished the chores just after seven o'clock. The night cold had coated the storm windows with an opaque glaze. When the phone rang, he answered curtly.

"Hiram Wainwright here, Porter. How are you tonight?"

"Same as I was last night. What's up?"

"We've decided to pay you the ten thousand for the land, Porter."

Porter didn't hesitate. "Price went to twenty just this afternoon."

Wainwright hesitated only a moment. "Then I guess we'll pay it, if you insist."

"State'll never go along with it."

"We're not talking about the state, Porter. The Merchants' Association is buying it. And we're going to *give* the land to the government."

Porter laughed. "You want that road in the worst way, don't you?"

"It will be good for all of us, Porter. I've heard you talking about wanting some dairy cattle before. Here's the money to get started."

"I've got my hands full with my hens."

"Then take the money and go on a vacation in Hawaii," Wainwright said.

"Can't stand humidity."

"It would do you some good."

"Don't worry about my health, Hiram."

"We all need to worry about each other's health. Economic *and* physical, too."

"Why? I'm happy to keep my nose out of *your* business."

"It ain't a question of having your nose where it doesn't belong, Porter. It's a question of helping each other."

"That road doesn't help me a damned bit. I don't pay that much attention to the summer business. And none of your friends in town want to buy my eggs lately. What do I need a road for?" Porter paced as far as the short telephone cord would let him.

"Just think about it, will you, Porter? Twenty thousand dollars. Five thousand down. Tonight. The rest in the morning."

Porter thought about the money for only a few minutes, then he thought about the fox. He tried to remember every move the fox had made. Where was the fox right now? Hadn't he, in fact, tried to flee? As Porter paced, he recalled Marion's accusation that he read too much into the things that went on around him. He retorted by telling her she was oblivious to what was going on around her.

He poured a cup of coffee, then sat at the table and thought about what the new road would mean, if he allowed it to be completed. He couldn't sit on his front porch anymore without having every out-of-stater who drove by stare at him. And now they thought they were going to run the cars right by his porch *railing* and raise the speed limit to fifty-five, which meant they'd go seventy. Twenty feet from his hammock.

When he opened the kitchen door to check the thermometer, the night chill stole in and made him shiver long after he had closed the door. He turned on two burners of the electric range and stood with his back to the stove a few minutes. He used to laugh at Marion when she did that. After he had gotten rid of the chill, he absently poured new coffee and milk into his cup, but the sight of the coffee made his stomach roll.

The fox had just limped off, he remembered. Wasn't that a sign of defeat?

Porter knew he couldn't take the twenty thousand dollars that Wainwright seemed willing to pay. The town would always hold it against him. He looked for his reflection in the window, but the gray-frosted glass returned nothing. He thought about going to bed, but sleep was nowhere in his body. He tried to remember when he'd last spent a night alone. Not in the army— there'd been nine other guys in his bay in the barracks. And not since he'd been married. Had he been hunting alone? He couldn't remember. All he could recall was Marion there in the tent with him, the two of them in his sleeping bag. She was so light when she laid her head on his chest.... Porter jumped when the phone rang. It was Hiram Wainwright again.

"Drove by your house a while ago, Porter. Looked like a lot of lights on for damn near midnight. I can't get to sleep, myself. Figured you were having the same problem."

"No problem at all, Hiram. Just a bunch of things to do."

"Listen, if you're afraid we're going to hold the money against you, forget it. We consider it an investment. You'll use the money well, probably start a dairy and expand your poultry operation. Maybe hire a few people. That's good for all of us, you know."

"Yeah, especially when you raise my taxes after the new road is finished."

Wainwright came back quickly. "Once this road is built, Porter, we'll never have to raise taxes again. Not local taxes, anyway."

Porter waited for him to continue. He didn't; only hung up. Porter listened to the hum of the phone line for several moments before he, too, hung up. He took his jacket from the back of a chair and sat down to put on a second pair of socks. He looked in the closet for a second scarf and for his flashlight.

Outside, the full moon cast its cold, gray light over the snow and the sleeping henhouse. Porter's snowshoes creaked in the crusty night snow. Halfway across the field he began to wonder if he should have brought his rifle, but he decided not to go back for it. Instead, he walked faster toward the woods. It was cold in the woods too. The night had frozen the water that had drained down the trunks all afternoon, and now the trees were ablaze

with the reflection of his flashlight. Ice had silenced the brook
for the night, and Porter came upon it sooner than he expected.
He stumbled once, but managed to hold up the powerful flashlight. His fence snagged him as he hurried through.

He was not ready for the wind that swirled across the lake,
taking his breath away the moment he emerged from the woods.
He felt as if he were being sliced down the middle, and his face
was instantly numb. He turned his back to the wind and
crouched, trying to figure out where he had watched the fox that
afternoon. The snow ghosts that the wind carried pelted his face
and twisted across the white sheet of the lake, whipping them-
selves to powder. As he began to feel his way out onto the lake,
the ice cracked far away and echoed its terrible thunder across
the whiteness until it was swallowed by the wind. He wandered
from drift to drift, poking expectantly with his foot. Still, he
was surprised when he came upon the dead animal, stiff on its
side. He watched only a moment as the wind made tiny furrows
in its fur. The idea of carrying the fox back to the house and
burying it in his yard passed through his mind, but he decided
against it.

Only if he'd shot the fox that afternoon, when he could have
saved it some suffering, would it make sense to bury it in his
yard. In sight of the chicken coop, maybe...

It was late, but he knew he could call her. He'd make hot
chocolate before she got home. The hot chocolate would give
them something to do with their hands and mouths so that he
wouldn't have to say much. And before long, it could even be
considered time for an early breakfast. He'd make pancakes, even
though it wasn't Sunday. And if they did talk, they could talk
about how they'd move the hammock to the back of the house
where the passing traffic couldn't see it. He looked at the fence
along the road one last time before he went inside and pictured
the field in the summer with one of the cows swatting at flies
with her tail.

All-You-Can-Eat Night

"I'm at your house all the time," Mack said. "Two, three nights a week. Least I can do is treat you both to a good eat once in a while."

Mack pulled his Buick into the parking lot, maneuvering in lunges and jerks around two other cars to grab a parking spot close to the door of the restaurant.

"Man, they pack 'em in on Thursday night, don't they? It's all-you-can-eat night, that's why."

As Mack turned the engine off he smiled, first at Kitty in the front seat, then at Maynard in the back.

Mack was burly and laughed too much, in Maynard's opinion, and Mack's public demonstrations of kindness at the department store where he and Mack worked together always struck Maynard as false. Mack pretended to be interested in their co-workers' kids, and he always volunteered to head up the Heart Fund or United Way drives. Maynard was a little surprised that Mack had invited them out on a Thursday night; that was Kitty's bowling night, and Maynard thought Mack went to an archery class at the YMCA on Thursdays. Maynard had come to count on Thursday as the one night of the week when he could be by himself and work out with the two small dumb-bells he kept hidden in the basement of their apartment building. He knew that working out only once a week did little to improve his health or physique—in fact, he ached for a week after working with the weights—but on that one night of the week, he felt that he at least had the potential to improve himself. To build up his arms to the size of Mack's.

Mack was Maynard's boss at the department store where they worked. Mack was the shipping clerk and Maynard was the assistant shipper. All day long Mack would play boss, telling Maynard to wrap this package a certain way or to send that package by

UPS rather than Airborne. But the moment the clock hit five, Mack became Maynard's best friend—Mr. Good Time, as Maynard called him around Kitty. Ever since Mack's wife died of cancer five years earlier, Mack had been coming around to Maynard's and Kitty's, frequently and uninvited.

Maynard struggled out of the back seat. He could tell that Kitty, even though she'd been quiet, was enjoying not having to cook. She and Maynard were both forty-one, ten years younger than Mack. Kitty, who worked as a secretary at Weight Watchers, was lean and sinewy with shoulder-length brown hair that caused her to stare at the mirror for hours and absently reel off the endless possibilities that she could do to transform her hair into something special, as she put it.

"Should I dye it blond?" she'd ask.

"It's fine the way it is."

"No it isn't. It's plain and ugly."

"Then change it."

"To what?"

"Anything you want."

"But I don't know what I want."

"Then don't change it."

And she didn't change it, but she seemed always to be thinking about changing something. In Maynard's opinion, she was neither good-looking nor bad—nor were her looks important to him. What had always attracted him most was her lethargic demeanor and air of boredom, even though he knew she took in everything. Days might pass before she mentioned something she had seen in a store window or some person in the park across the street from their apartment building.

Mack always gave Kitty plenty of attention, and when they went out, people assumed that Kitty was Mack's wife because of the way Mack made her take his arm, and the way he always rushed ahead to open doors for her.

"May I borrow your wife, Good Buddy?" Mack would say. "Just her arm, I mean. Ha ha...."

Maynard sensed that Kitty liked the attention Mack paid her, even though she often complained about Mack when he wasn't around.

"He's so pushy," she'd say about Mack. "He wants what he wants when he wants it, even though he smiles real nice while he's wanting it."

Although Mack was stout and clumsy, Maynard had to concede that he was very good looking for fifty-one—dark-haired, dark-eyed, perfect teeth.

Mack held the door open, and Maynard and Kitty went into the crowded, noisy restaurant. The house music was late Fifties stuff, and Mack did a few steps of The Twist. Kitty patted his arm and made a tiny, gulping laugh.

Mr. Good Time, Maynard thought scornfully.

The hostess led them to a table, and Mack pulled Kitty's chair out for her. Maynard could see that Mack was very pleased with himself to be taking them out and wondered if Mack considered this one meal to be payment for the fifteen or twenty meals they'd fed Mack since the last time he took them out.

"You *know* how I love to eat,"Mack said. His conversation seemed always directed at Kitty. "I mean, I *love* to eat." He held his midsection between his hands. "And look at this. No gut whatsoever."

Poor Kitty, Maynard thought. A rare night out to eat and she has to listen to Mack talk about how wonderful he is.

"Now I want you two to have a drink," Mack said. "All the drinks you want, in fact. And then..."He nodded toward the several buffet counters. "...And then I want you to eat everything you want." He touched Kitty's wrist. "You don't need that menu, Darlin'; everything you want is right over yonder."

Kitty pouted. "Oh, you mean I *have* to have the buffet?"

Mack drew back in his seat but kept his hand on Kitty's wrist. "No no. Have anything you want. It's just me and Maynard who's got to have the buffet. You can have that Greek-style lamb if you want." Mack moved his chair closer to her. "The prime rib. The lobster...."

"Oh.... Then I want the lobster," Kitty said.

Mack slapped the table with a wild, sweeping gesture, although his hand hardly made a sound on the tablecloth. "It's yours!"

A waitress came to the table, forced a haggard smile, and stood with her pad ready.

"How y'all doing tonight? Everybody want the buffet?"

"Hungry," said Mack. "And thirsty."

"Maybe I'll have lobster, too," Maynard said.

"Unh unh. You and me are having the buffet, Good Buddy. It's fabulous. You'll see. All you can eat."

"But...I'm not all that hungry."

"Then have the salad bar," Mack said. "That's an all you-can-eat deal, too."

"I don't know...that lobster sounds mighty good...."

"Oh, Maynard," Kitty said, pouting. "The last time you had lobster, you hated it, remember? It was when we were at that motel in..."

"I loved it," Maynard said quickly. "It was the salad bar I didn't like."

"Do you want me to come back in a little while?" the waitress asked.

"No," Mack said. "We're ready. Two buffets and a lobster for the little lady. And bring us a big ole pitcher of them margaritas and three salty glasses."

Maynard had disliked Mack all day, but now he hated him. Again. On Tuesday night, when Mack ate at Maynard's house, Mack had jumped up afterward and insisted on doing the dishes. Kitty said,

"That's awfully nice of you, Mack. Maynard *never* does the dishes." The next night, Mack told Kitty about how Maynard had made a pass at Lilian, the girl who worked the lingerie counter at the department store. Maynard insisted that it was not a pass, and Mack just laughed and said that no, it wasn't a pass because Lilian turned him down.

"In football, it's what we used to call an *incomplete* pass, Good Buddy."

Kitty laughed at the time, but as soon as Mack was gone, she turned sullen and silent. She fell asleep on the couch, reading, and Maynard woke up in the middle of the night wondering where she was. When he found her, he covered her with two blankets and went back to bed.

Mack patted Maynard's arm. "Ready to chow down there, Good Buddy? Or you want to have a drink first?"

"Yes, I thought we were going to drink first," Kitty said.

That worried Maynard. She didn't often drink, not at home anyway, and could get tipsy on a single screwdriver, which was her favorite thing to drink. On two, she had to be carried home, and then she would spend the rest of the night throwing up or tossing around in bed and crying over some long-dead relative. The pitcher of margaritas arrived, and Mack proceeded to pour. Maynard never drank when Kitty did, but tonight he was torn between spending Mack's money and keeping an eye on Kitty. He put his hand over the top of his glass just as Mack lifted the pitcher toward him.

"No thanks. Not tonight."

"Oh, come on," Mack urged. "Drink up. T'son me."

"Good," Kitty said. "I'll just drink one for him. And then one for myself. It's been a hard week."

Here we go, thought Maynard. Now we'll hear all about how much Linda and Grace hate her and how everytime Kitty comes back into the office, they're whispering about her. They never seemed to actually *do* anything to her, but they were always whispering about her. Maynard got so sick of hearing Kitty's complaining that he'd told her a couple of weeks ago that he didn't want to hear it anymore. In return, Maynard agreed not to talk about the department store.

"Those two witches at your office bugging you again?" Mack asked.

She glanced at Maynard. "I don't want to talk about it."

Mack laughed and sat back in his chair, tipping his salty glass up. When he set it down again, his upper lip was coated with light green foam. "That's right....no shop talk. I always forget." He tapped one of his large, hairy fingers on the back of his over-turned spoon. After a few moments he stopped that and began drumming on the table, his loud fingernails galloping in what made Maynard think of the Lone Ranger theme—and also made him wonder how Mack knew about the ban on talking about work.

Maynard sipped his Coke and tuned out the conversation between Mack and Kitty. He thought about Lilian the lingerie girl. What he liked about Lilian was that she seemed genuinely curious about people. She was always caked with makeup and didn't seem intelligent at first, but when they happened to sit together in the break room, she asked Maynard questions about himself that nobody else had ever asked. Like what he did when he got home from work. Lilian wanted to know his first three acts upon walking in the door. Then she wanted to know his first three acts when he woke up in the morning, and if he ever had recurring dreams. She never used the questions to turn the conversation to herself—it was pure curiosity, Maynard had come to realize. But Mack had already spread it all over the store that Maynard was trying to put a move on Lilian. Other people, especially the women in the store, talked about Lilian too, suggesting that she was far worse than merely flirtatious. Maynard figured it was because Lilian seldom talked to the women. She'd told Maynard that women just didn't interest her very much.

"I already know what makes women tick," she said. "I want to know about men."

"But you're thirty-seven.... Haven't you figured men out by now?"

"God, no.... I know less than I did when I was eighteen," she said. "Back then it seemed obvious what men were all about. What boys are all about anyway."

"So what have you learned lately about men?"

"Probably the same things you've learned about women," was all she said. With that little grin of hers. That was the last time they talked. Mack and the others had made it impossible for Maynard to talk to Lilian anymore.

*****

Maynard eyed the drink in Kitty's hand. What the hell, he thought, if she wants to get plastered, let her. She only does it once or twice a year. Maynard wondered if Kitty would drink more if he were to suddenly die. He'd heard of women who became alcoholics after their husbands died. He could see Kitty becoming a lush out of sheer loneliness. He could see her starting out with a bottle to come home to at night, but sooner or later heading out for the bars. Both her parents and her sister lived in Seattle. There would be no family members to report her behavior to other family members.

What *would* she do? She had hobbies—needlework and furniture refinishing and bowling—but what meaning could they hold when your husband dies, he wondered. Most women Maynard had met who had lost their husbands were bent on finding another husband. None of them stayed home to crochet. They went out to card games and fund raisers and church, or they took night courses at the university to meet people. He couldn't see Kitty taking courses. She had never talked about taking courses. Just what would she do? He'd known her for twenty-two years, been married to her for nineteen, but he had no idea what she'd do if he died.

Maynard could see it was time to rescue her from Mack, who was going on and on about crossword puzzles. He was saying that he loved learning all those new words, but Maynard had never heard Mack use a new word.

"I see where they finally got the funds approved for that new expressway connection," Maynard said. Kitty and Mack looked at him as if he were speaking from a television. Maynard thought he should add something, if that wasn't a topic they might bite for. "...And they caught a suspect in that pet store robbery case. You know, the one that's been stealing all the parrots?"

Mack and Kitty looked down at their drinks. Maynard knew he'd succeeded in disrupting their conversation but not in turning it. He tried to think of something quickly, before they began again with the crossword puzzles.

"I saw on the TV the other night that if they don't start killing some of the people on death row, the prisons are going to be more overcrowded than they've ever been. But school enrollment is down, and they may just convert some of those baby-boom schools they built in the fifties into prisons."

Kitty laughed. "I always thought *my* school looked like a prison!"

Mack once again lifted the margarita pitcher toward Maynard's glass. "Good Buddy...you got to help us with these margaritas. It ain't like you to pass up a free drink."

Maynard pulled his glass away, and Mack spilled a bit on the table. "No, please, I really don't..."

Mack seemed annoyed. "Well hell, you don't have to waste it."

The waitress brought Kitty's salad, and Mack pushed back his chair and nodded at Maynard. "C'mon, we got us some serious eating to do. Let's get started."

At the salad bar, Maynard felt almost hungry as he picked up a plate and heaped it high with lettuce and cherry tomatoes and even the bean sprouts, which looked crisp and cool. He decided to try the croutons and bacon bits and everything he'd never wanted to put on a salad—black olives, anchovies, beets.

"You can come back for anything you want," Mack said, as if he owned the place.

They moved down the line to the vegetables and entrees. Maynard watched Mack heap two plates with roast beef and hamburger steak and ham, a third plate with fried catfish and porkchops, and a fourth with peach cobbler, fried apple pie, and banana pudding. Mack looked serious, nearly pained as he informed Maynard that he'd have to come back for that last plate.

"Unless just the sight of all this good grub makes me grow a third hand!"

Back at the table, Mack arranged his plates in front of him and tasted a bite from each. "Exquisite," he called the hamburger steak. "Savory," he said of the ham. The catfish was "crisp and juicy," and the fried chicken was "finger-lickin' good. Just like the Colonel's, only better."

Savory was a new word, Maynard thought. From the cross-words?

"You know," Mack went on, "when I was a young fella, seems I used to couldn't stay away from those I-can-eat-anything contests they have at the country fairs. You know those contests?" He continued to fork bites from each of his plates. "I'll tell you, I won a couple of those suckers, but I'll never forget the first time I lost. You know what I couldn't eat? This may sound like the damnedest thing. And I'm telling you right now, don't ever say you can eat it. Especially if you wind up in a I-can-eat-anything contest.

"It was instant coffee. I put a big tablespoon of that stuff in my mouth, and I swear to God I could *not* get it down." Mack slapped the table and leaned back on the two hind legs of his chair. "I mean, raw eggs, shell and all, straight vinegar, cold bacon grease. I used to could eat *anything*. But that instant coffee brought me right to my knees." Mack laughed and slapped the table as he shoveled in a slice of roast beef and kept talking as he chewed.

"Lard, orange peels, parsley? I swear to God I used to could eat anything...."

Maynard chewed at his salad, but he didn't taste it. He'd lost the small twinge of appetite he'd felt. He wondered what Kitty was thinking about. She hadn't even begun her salad. Maynard noticed that she was half way through her second margarita. She held the drink in a distant, thoughtful kind of way—like you'd see a woman holding a drink on the cover of a Sinatra album. Twenty years with her and he didn't even know what she was thinking. The idea angered him for just a second, then saddened him.

When she suddenly downed the rest of the drink, the motion startled him.

"I'd like another," she announced.

Maynard's first reaction was to caution her, but he kept his mouth shut lest Mack accuse him of trying to stifle her. She didn't seem drunk, after all. Just quiet. Maybe the drinks would catch up to her before the lobster came and make her realize she'd had enough. Mack was bent low over his plate, shoving slices of ham and pineapple into his mouth.

"Anything you like," he said. "Drink up. T'son me. And you, Good Buddy, you hurting my feelings by being a teetotaler when the drinks are free."

Maynard smiled inside, realizing once again that Mack was a plain slob. Maynard started to eat his own food, but slowly and with restraint, so that Kitty might notice and appreciate the contrast with Mack. But she wasn't noticing anything. She looked across the restaurant at nothing. Maynard suddenly wanted to tell Kitty all about work, even about Lilian, and how it was when Mack tried to order him around, and when the department heads bitched about the mailroom not getting their customers' orders out quickly enough, and how the three senile brothers who owned the store came through the shipping room sixteen times a day to ask the same questions over and over.

"Ready for more, Good Buddy?"

Maynard took a small bite of his roast beef and shook his head.

Mack smiled. "Not hardly, huh?"

Mack pushed his chair back and stood up with his three empty plates. "I am, by God...."

Maynard waited until Mack was out of earshot. "What a slob, huh?"

"We're all slobs of one kind or another," Kitty said absently.

"Look, what's eating you? Is it that business with the lingerie girl at the store that Mack mentioned? That was strictly...I mean, it's just *intellectual*, kind of."

She turned toward him and laughed. "*Intellectual*? I've never heard you use that word in your life."

Maynard tried to continue to eat slowly and deliberately, as if to prove that he enjoyed his food far more than Mack did.

"Can I get you anything?" the waitress asked. Maynard's hand jumped at her sudden presence. He noticed her look at Kitty's untouched salad.

"Want me to tell the cook to slow down on that lobster?"

"No," Kitty said. "I'll eat sooner or later. I don't mind if it gets a little bit cold."

The waitress left, and Maynard offered her a morsel on his fork. "Want to taste this smoked turkey?"

"Not really."

"Not in a turkey mood?"

"I'm not in any mood...."

"But we've got to spend Mack's money."

"Oh Maynard, grow up. It's not the first time he ever took us out."

"No, it may actually be the second."

"Come on.... He takes us out once or twice a month. I guess you don't remember because you usually wind up so drunk it takes the two of us to carry you up the stairs and put you to bed."

"Well...I'm sober as a judge tonight."

Kitty looked at him with her small, sad smile. "I know. And that's the problem."

Mack was back with three more plates of food, mostly vegetables this time. Maynard instinctively glanced at Mack's stomach. Mack noticed and patted his belly.

"You'd think I'd have a big ole gut, wouldn't you?"

Maynard thought of several replies but decided to say nothing. He was about to ask Kitty why it was a problem that he was not drunk, but the waitress brought the lobster just then, and Kitty watched the plate with such intensity that the moment seemed too solemn to be interrupted by what might have been an unanswerable question.

"Eat up, you two. Neither one of you are going to get your money's worth at the rate you're going. *My* money's worth, that is. And *damn*, Good Buddy...you supposed to be drunk by now!"

"I am?"

"I'm doing it *for* you," Kitty said. She reached to pat Maynard's hand

"I can't believe you're not wolfing that roast beef right down," Mack said. "And the turkey breast is downright *sapid*. Ha ha. Bet you ain't never heard that word before, right?"

Maynard realized that he wanted to be home, reading in bed with Kitty, or doing the dishes from breakfast—something that might please her. Before they fell asleep that night, he would certainly tell her that he never meant for them to get like this, that they used to talk so well together when they were younger, and that he'd never again tell her she couldn't talk about what it was like for her at work.

*****

When she'd eaten about half of her lobster, Kitty set her napkin down and asked Maynard if he had any money.

"Yeah...two, three bucks. Why? You're the one that carries the money...."

She reached across the table, hand open. "I want to buy a pack of cigarettes. I left my purse in the car."

Maynard waited for Mack to offer to buy the cigarettes, and when that didn't happen, Maynard pulled out his wallet and gave

her a five, which was the last of his week's lunch money. Kitty
left the table.

"She clean you out, Good Buddy?"

"Basically...."

"Every last dime?"

"I got about sixty cents."

Mack laughed. "Then she didn't do it right, did she? Heh
heh..." Mack continued to shovel food into his wide, grinding
jaws. Maynard watched in silence. He jumped when Mack's pager
went off with its loud, frantic beep. Mack stopped chewing long
enough to glance at the number panel, then swallowed.

"Damn. It's the store. Hope it ain't a fire or something. You
unplug the coffee pot, Good Buddy?"

"Yeah. Pretty sure."

As he watched Mack cross the dining room Maynard felt a
moment of disorientation and wondered where he was. His food
looked a week old, and Kitty's unfinished lobster smelled like
the fish canneries down by the docks. How had this happened,
Maynard wondered? How had he allowed himself to stay in that
same store with nothing in the world for him to look forward to
except Mack? How had he allowed things to arrive at the point
where all he did was come home at night and watch television
while Kitty cooked frozen dinners? At least he'd always done
the floors and the bathroom and the laundry. That was to his
credit, wasn't it? And he built her a loom last year when she
thought she wanted to take up weaving. And he built her that
nice china cabinet for her birthday ten or twelve years ago.

But what else had he done? His memory clouded, and he remembered his grandmother, who had always said how smart he
was. He was glad she was not around to see what he had not
become.

*****

Maynard realized that Mack and Kitty had been gone for
awhile, and he wondered where they were. He glanced at his
watch. It was going on ten, but he really had no idea what time
they'd left the table. Most of the tables were now empty, and
Maynard sensed that it was near closing time. He looked at Kitty's
four empty margarita glasses and at Mack's stack of plates, the
top one still piled high with scalloped potatoes and fried corn.
Maynard wished there were some way to sprinkle the food with
coffee grounds, to conceal the coffee grounds somewhere so that
Mack would have them in his mouth and clogged against his

throat before he even knew what he was eating. Maynard chuckled to himself before he noticed the waitress.

"You all right, Hon?"

Maynard looked around to see if anyone else had noticed. "Fine," he managed to say. "Where's the bathroom?"

He did not find Mack in the men's room. He waited outside the ladies' room until someone came out, and he asked her if there was anyone else inside. She looked at Maynard suspiciously and said no. When he got back to the table, he found the waitress leaving a note.

"From Mack somebody. Says he had to go into the store, and that your wife got sick and he was going to drop her off at home on the way. Said he'd be back to pick you up in a little while."

Like hell, Maynard thought. He rose from the table and headed for the cashier's desk.

"Can you call me a cab?" he said to her.

The cashier looked at him over her glasses as if he were a child. "If you'll wait just a minute. You made me lose count."

Maynard watched her count, thinking to himself that Mack had one hell of a nerve to just take Kitty with him.

"Where's there a phone?" Maynard demanded.

The cashier refused to answer. Maynard headed out the door. There was no directory in the phone booth outside, so he called information and jotted the number of the cab company along his index finger. The cab arrived before Maynard had even paced the length of the parking lot.

"Where to?" The cabbie's hair was gray, and his face ruddy and deeply creased. He looked so intently at Maynard in the mirror that Maynard moved over in the seat, out of the mirror's range. When they were in front of his apartment building, Maynard saw that there were no lights on upstairs.

"Here you are," said the cabbie.

Maynard fumbled in his pockets before he remembered that Kitty had taken all of his money for cigarettes.

"I'm gonna have to run upstairs to get some money. If you don't mind."

The cabbie did mind, Maynard could tell. Tough shit. You want to get paid, you wait. But when Maynard opened the apartment door and called for Kitty, no one answered, and he quickly found that the apartment was empty. At first alarmed then angry, he hurried back down to the cab and got in. He gave the cabbie Mack's address.

The cabbie nodded and drove. "Big guy?" he asked.

Maynard moved to see the cabbie's face in the mirror. "Yeah."

"I know who you mean. He comes down to that all-you-can-eat deal almost every Thursday night. Missed him tonight. He usually has his girlfriend with him."

"Girlfriend?"

"Oh yeah. They go crazy there in the back seat. I never seen nothing like it. And I've seen some stuff, believe me. This pair is the strangest, though. She's always carrying a bowling ball, and he's always carrying a goddam bow and arrow. I call him Robin Hood and he calls me James Cagney. She's real quiet—never says a word." The cabbie smiled into the mirror. "People tell me I look like Cagney."

They were on Mack's street. There was Mack's Buick, but there were no lights on in his apartment windows. Maynard looked up at the darkened windows for a few moments, then told the cab driver to just drive. Maynard didn't care whether he had money or not. The cabbie could turn him over to the cops, if it came to that.

The cabbie was still talking about how much he looked like James Cagney, and how years ago before the actor died, the cabbie used to drive out to the airport dressed up kind of casual but sharp and just hang around. Sure enough, someone would come up to him and ask if he was Cagney and then ask for an autograph.

"I'd quote some movie line, then sign whatever they had. Matchbooks, napkins...you name it."

Maynard said nothing. He tried to breathe quietly so that the cabbie wouldn't notice. His insides felt crusted and dry, and he was not surprised that he felt no inclination to cry. The cab coasted slowly along a street lined with apartment buildings like the one he and Kitty lived in.

"Where is it you want to go exactly?"

"I dunno. Airport, maybe. I'd like to see you in action."

"Cagney's dead. Nobody recognizes me anymore."

"I do."

The cabbie's smile grew toward one side. He watched the street now instead of Maynard, and he let his foot settle harder on the accelerator. "Ten minutes, fifteen at the most," he said. "If nobody asks me for an autograph, we're outta there."

Roland Fogg

Roland had been at the gravel pit for fourteen hours, since six o'clock that morning, and they still hadn't finished for the day. Tomorrow would be just as bad, and most of the crew would be working long hours for at least two more weeks. Roland's old dump truck shuddered as the loader heaped on another three-yard scoop of the sandy soil that covered the layers of gray rock they would dynamite next week and feed to the rock crushers.

Roland eased the worn clutch out slowly, but the truck jumped forward anyway, throwing him a little off balance as he tried to slip the shifting lever into second without grinding it. The transmission made its usual feeble clang, and Roland glanced at Pike, the foreman, who glared back from his dented old yellow Caddy convertible. Pike had pulled out in front of Roland as he left for the day. Pike was never the last one to leave, and he was no help when he was here, just sitting in that convertible and watching everybody through his reflecting sunglasses. Following him now down the road that wound among the pyramids of gravel, Roland could see Pike watching every move in his rear-view mirror. Pike drove slowly, just to irk him, Roland knew. Roland downshifted to maintain a few car-lengths behind the rusted Cadillac. Just before the curve where Roland turned onto the logging path where they were dumping that week, Pike sped off, kicking up dust and pebbles that flew in through Roland's window as he made his turn.

As soon as Pike was gone, Roland felt the tension leave him. He turned on his headlights in the dim pine woods, although the sky was still bright blue just above the tree tops. He had been more cautious since the beginning of the week, when Pike accused him of denting a fender on his already battered truck.

The mosquitoes hovered in the open cab and buzzed near

Roland's ears. He had long ago given up slapping at them, nor did he scratch the bites they left. That seemed futile. Easier, he decided, to refuse to recognize them, just as he ignored the beads of sweat that trickled along his skull and down his cheeks and neck, leaking from his brows into his hot, tired eyes. Roland suspected it was Pike himself who had dented the truck and was trying to pin it on someone else. Roland had watched the way Pike drove, shaving off the piles of gravel rather than maneuvering around them. Roland had observed everyone at the quarry and concluded that he was the best driver Pike had.

Pike had also badgered Roland for losing a gas cap and a dipstick and for allowing the truck to run out of gas in the woods—things that had nothing to do with being a good driver, as Roland saw it. He'd explained that the gas gauge said the tank was half full. Pike argued that everybody knew that the gas gauge in that truck didn't work.

The harassment had been going on for some time, over two weeks, Roland figured, since the night when Pike had come back to the pit just before quitting time looking for someone to help him with his cow. Only Otis and Roland had stayed late, and Otis's wife was already there waiting, the flesh of her neck jiggling as she sat in the unmuffled, idling Ford, and her dimpled elbow hanging out over the door in a V. Three children with smudged faces and shaved heads peered out the back window at Pike.

Roland, dog-tired and grimey from the long day, had known at a glance that he would be the one who had to go with Pike.

They drove in silence to Pike's farm, two miles away. Turn on the headlights, goddamn it, Roland had thought, fidgeting in the passenger seat as they bounded over the gouged road. Even with the top down, the inside of the old Cadillac smelled like dog piss. The dust swirled about them when Pike screeched the car to a halt in his barnyard, and Roland gagged rather than let himself cough. From outside the barn they could hear the bleating cow thrash about in her stall. Some of the other cows answered with alarmed grunts, then quieted suddenly when Roland and Pike entered the barn. Pike's feet made a sharp, hateful thud on the hay-matted floor. At the far end of the darkened barn, a bare lightbulb hung from a cord above the suffering cow's stall.

"I called the vet," Pike said as they walked. "He said to give her a shot and reach in there and pull them calves out by hand."

They came first upon the cow's hindquarters as she leaned against one side of the stall, her sides bulging with dead calves. Pike's head bumped against the lightbulb, and in the now swaying light, Roland began to feel nauseous as he caught his first glimpse of a glistening head, or part of one, that protruded from the cow's posterior.

"C'mon," Pike said, picking up a long hypodermic needle from the floor. He pointed toward the cow's tossing head and wild eyes. "Lean her good and hard against that wall. Hold her tight."

Roland tried to push the cow against the wall, but just touching the cows rough hide gave him the willies. Pike didn't seem to notice. He braced his shoulder against the cow and plunged the needle into its neck. The cow wrenched hard once, nearly throwing Pike across the stall, but he lunged back and stabbed the needle even more deeply into the frantic, braying cow. When the needle was empty, Pike prepared another injection. The cow's reaction to the second needle was more subdued, and Roland took a step backward and watched the muscle spasms that rippled down the cow's back.

"I'll pin her against the wall," Pike wheezed, "and you pull that calf outta there." Roland watched the cow's head twist and felt the cow's strength as she tried to break free of Pike. Roland tried to say something but couldn't speak.

"*Pull*, goddamn it!"

Roland looked at the wet crown that had lodged itself in the cow's torn, bleeding orifice. The blood ran freely down her leg into the muddy discharge on the floor. Roland's eyes clouded with the ammonium stench, but he made his hand reach out to the dead fetus and touch its filmy surface.

"There ain't nothin' to grab...."

Pike twisted around so that he could maintain his headlock and at the same time, drive his elbow into the cow's bulging side. The cow brayed loudly when Pike threw all his weight against her. The rest of the calf's head burst into the open as the cow's hind legs buckled, knocking Roland to the stinking, slimy floor. Even after he had fainted, he could still feel the light dangling over him like a desert sun.

He awakened there at daybreak and found the stall empty and the light no longer swaying. He stared at it for several moments as he recalled the events of the night, then he forced himself to stand on his shaky legs. His clothes were soggy with liquid filth, his bare arms and hands caked. He didn't even consider waking Pike up to ask him for a ride home. Instead, Roland stumbled through the barn, then through the pasture, instantly sweating in the already hot sun, into the woods beyond Pike's land.

When he was out of sight of the house, Roland peeled off his dungarees and shirt and dragged them, tied in his belt. He stopped at the brook and dunked the clothes, then left them to rinse in a place where the water rushed over the rocks with enough force to make a foam. He washed himself upstream from his clothes. His boots filled with water as he stood in the stream, and he worked his feet inside them to flush the water between his toes. He left his clothes rinsing in the brook and trudged the two miles home, naked but for the boots that coughed and sucked at his heels with each step.

The unusual heat had caused his cabin to smell bad, or so he thought. It could have been the stench of the cow birth that he'd carried home with him. Roland shoved a crumpled sheet of newspaper, a fistful of twigs, and four small logs of green pine into his stove and lit a fire. He went to the well outside to draw water into buckets for a bath. It would take at least an hour for the water to heat. As he waited, Roland made the mistake of lying down for a short rest and didn't wake up until the bath water had all boiled away and the four galvanized pails had turned black. The sun was already high, and his eyes throbbed behind his parched eyelids.

It was well after noon when Roland arrived at work, and Pike had already left for the day. But the following day, Pike's relentless stare stalked him every time Roland looked up from what he was doing. It had been like that for a week, Roland mused. Never saying anything, but just staring and spitting in my direction. Like tonight, pulling out in front of me and then slowing down.

Just to bust my balls.

*****

Roland felt the axle scrape the ridge in the middle of the road. When they'd begun dumping in the ravine at the end of the abandoned logging road, there had been a lush green spine of grass down the middle, but the heavy dumptrucks had quickly worn the ruts deeper and shaved away the grass. Now the road was as parched and dry as the quarry pit itself.

The logging path broke into a field, and Roland stepped harder on the accelerator and bounced toward the edge of the ravine. He deftly whipped the truck around and backed toward the edge of the dumping pit. He thought about Pike again and how Pike would have been jerking the truck as he backed up— and then wouldn't have had the nerve to get close enough to the edge to get the load into the ravine. Otis or Carl would have to come out there with the bulldozer and push it off. Roland had heard the men say that the only reason Pike was foreman was that he had married the owner's daughter in a shotgun wedding, only the shotgun was being held to old man Walsh's head, not Pike's.

Roland inched a little closer to the edge, then stopped. The truck swayed for a moment on its ancient springs. When he jumped out to unfasten the tailgate hitch, he was surprised at how close he was to the edge. It was a forty-foot drop to the bottom, a boulder-strewn hillside with a much steeper bank on the other side. He wondered if he really was too close to the edge, or if he was just spooked because he was alone in the woods at night.

He climbed back into the truck to pull forward, but as the rear wheels began to dig, the bank gave way. Roland knew in an instant that he was going down. His stomach rose into his throat as the truck pitched down the hillside, hurling him from one door to the other, against the roof, against the windshield.

He waited for the truck to roll over but it didn't. When it came to rest against a boulder, Roland was flung for a final time against the back of his seat. The dust rushed into the cab of the truck. He didn't dare move for fear the truck would tumble the rest of the way down the incline—maybe flip this time.

Another thought entered his mind, that the gas tank might explode if the truck were to collide with anything. Small stones and chunks of the bank continued to pelt the truck, and Roland began to fear that something large enough to smash the windshield would come hurtling through the dust and glass into his lap.

He began to inch himself closer to the door and held his breath as he lifted the handle. He felt no movement of the truck, but he jumped well clear of it just in case. He backed away, waving and coughing at the dust. He was relieved to see that the truck was closer to the bottom than he'd suspected, cradled between a boulder and one of the few trees left on the bank. Even standing on firm ground, Roland still felt the truck tumbling around him. He collapsed and let himself breathe and tremble.

No need to worry about working at Walsh's Gravel Pit any more, he knew. Pike's lips would tighten, and and his jowls would twitch as he looked at the truck, spat, and told Roland to get out of his sight. That's what he told guys when he fired them, to get out of his sight.

As night drifted into the ravine, Roland looked at the truck's dark form and decided that if the gas tank were going to blow up, it would have done it by now. And that the seat of the truck would be a safer place to sleep than the rocky bottom of the dumping pit, especially once the racoons started to roam.

*****

Morning came to Roland's ears and he remembered without opening his eyes where he was. He heard voices—Otis's he thought, or Carl's.

"Yeah, there he is. Jesus, he looks dead!"

More sand and rocks popped against the truck's grille as the men descended the bank. Roland didn't move. He tried not to breathe. The door opened and he felt a hand on his shoulder. He recognized Pike's voice.

"He's warm yet. Must be alive."

Pike burrowed his arms under Roland and grunted as he lifted him out of the truck. Roland had not yet decided what to do, so he kept his eyes closed and let himself go limp. Pike grunted again as he set Roland ungently on the ground.

"Jesus," Otis said. "What are we gonna do, take him to the Bangor hospital?"

"Hell no," Pike whined. "I got insurance regulations I gotta go by. You two stay here with him and I'll go call the state cops."

"His face sure got bashed," Otis droned.

Roland felt a momentary snap of panic, but when he searched his face for pain he found none.

"He may be too far gone," Pike said. "They'll have to bring an ambulance. Don't tell the cops I lifted him out like that. Just say we found him here on the ground if they ask you. And hook some chains up to the bulldozer and pull that truck back up while you're waiting for me to come back."

"Don't you think we oughta do somethin' with him?" Otis asked.

"Don't touch him," Pike said. "You'll be liable."

In the silence that was punctuated by Pike's fading footsteps, Roland felt the eyes of Otis and Carl.

"Christ, don't he look awful?" Otis groaned. "I'll bet he sues old man Walsh for a bundle."

"You think so?"

"Hell yes. Specially if he's hurt real bad. He'll get a bundle."

"You think so? How much?"

"Depends. I read once about a fella sued for five hundred thou for head damage. Claimed the accident made him retarded."

Roland heard them walking toward the truck, and he opened his eyes before he realized that Otis was looking back at him as they walked. Roland froze and stared ahead, beyond Otis and Carl.

"Holy Mother of Jesus. "

"What's the matter?" Carl asked.

"I just been stared at by a dead man....Their eyes open when they die, you know!"

Roland could see the terror on their faces and wondered what he looked like—if he really did look dead. Otis and Carl kept backing toward the truck as they stared. Roland wished they would turn away so he could move a leg that had gone to sleep. Two stones dug into his back, one under his spine and another under his shoulder blade.

"Whatta we do now?" Carl asked.

"I dunno. Wait, I guess."

Roland watched them stare, neither man blinking. When Roland could no longer stand the growing numbness in his legs, he moaned and shifted slightly. Carl's hand went to his mouth, and Otis's eyes widened, but neither moved. Roland stirred some more and sat up with his back to them.

"Roland?" Otis called feebly. "You all right?"

Roland didn't answer.

"Musta 'fected his brain," Otis whispered. "He'll sue for a bundle."

Roland turned his head slowly and again stared beyond them. Carl gulped, and Otis's hands went out behind him toward the door of the truck.

"He might be possessed," Otis said. "He looks kinda possessed to me...."

Carl peered harder. "What's possessed look like?"

Roland stood up in a single, sudden motion, and Otis and Carl shrieked as they stumbled around to the other side of the truck and watched from there. Roland squatted and continued to stare in their direction as his hands felt around him for a few rocks, which he gathered in a pile in front of him.

"Quick, inside the truck," Otis said. They piled in and rolled up the windows.

Roland continued to gather rocks, piling them neatly. Otis and Carl watched him with wide eyes, their heads just above the bottom of the window.

"He's buildin' somethin," he heard Carl say.

"Just like a little kid," Otis said. "But don't let that fool ya. A crazy man ain't like a little kid. They say a crazy man's got the strength of ten grown men."

"You think so?"

"I know so."

Roland stopped gathering rocks and stared at the truck.

"Oh God, he's lookin' at us again! Oh, God...he's comin' this way!"

Roland crawled forward until he knew they could no longer see him. The sun already burned, and the shade cast by the truck was an oasis.

"Where is he now?"

"I dunno. I guess he's under the truck."

"Oh no...he'll get us yet...he's got the strength of ten men!"

Through the rusted floorboards, Roland smiled at Carl's whimpering. He thought he heard car doors slam. Then he heard dirt and stones splatter down onto the truck.

"It's Pike," Otis squealed. "With a cop...let's make a run for it!"

The truck bounced as Otis and Carl scrambled out, and rust flakes fell onto Roland's face and into his hair. He watched their legs scurry up the hill.

"He's gone crazy," Carl hollered as he ran.

"Whaa...?"

"He tried to kill us," Otis said. "Crash 'fected his head."

"Where is he?" Pike boomed.

"Under the truck."

More gravel pelted the truck as Pike and the officer descended the bank. In moments, Roland could see the cop's boots. His knees dipped to the ground, then his round, sagging face appeared.

"Hey, can you hear me?" the trooper asked.

Roland nodded weakly.

"Can you make it out from under there?"

Roland said nothing but slowly rolled out from under the truck. He stood up, shaky on his legs, and extended his arms in front of him as he stared past Pike, who frowned. Roland felt the officer's hand close around his biceps. Otis and Carl parted before them. Two rescue workers were descending the bank with a stretcher.

"I want you all to come with me," the officer said. "I'll need to write up a full incident report."

Roland stopped abruptly, his arms still out in front of him, flailing slightly, as if he were sleepwalking. As he waited for the paramedics, he made his teeth chatter—a trick he'd learned in seventh grade, when his classmates were learning to burp, fart, or turn utterly ashen at will. When the paramedics touched Roland, he jumped. Then he allowed them to lower his arms to his sides and fold him down onto the stretcher.

Gone with Wind—Be Back Soon

It was Lincoln Webster's fifty-second birthday, and almost everyone who lived at the Hacienda Apartments was at Link's place, which was a one-room cellar apartment around the back of the beige, fake-Spanish building, the best Link could afford on disability. The cement floor was covered with several thin, threadbare rugs that various neighbors had found discarded on the sidewalk for the trash collectors to pick up. The light-green stucco walls displayed Link's parade of taped-up cut-outs from various girlie magazines. The pin-ups were blotted and blistered with water-damage from the fire the week before, and the black odor of smoke clung to the walls and scatter rugs, mixing with the smell of fresh paint that Landlord Larry had slapped on the floor and ceiling as well as the walls as soon as the insurance people had finished making their photos. The odors didn't bother Link; he claimed he hadn't been able to smell anything since the Korean War, thirty-two years ago.

He'd been in Birmingham about three years and had lived at The Hacienda almost the entire time—when he wasn't in and out of the VA de-tox program. He insisted that he was named after the car, not that friggin' war criminal who sent the generals to burn down as much of the South as they could.

"Besides," Link liked to tell Southerners, "my people all took off to Canada when the Civil War broke out."

His greasy, graying hair hung to his shoulders, and whisps stuck out at sharp angles above his ears. In his thick-lensed glasses and his still-black, mustacheless beard, he indeed looked a bit like Abraham Lincoln—a cross between Lincoln and a big-eyed tropical fish staring from an aquarium. Although everyone at Hacienda agreed that Link was basically a garden-variety drunk, they also agreed that there was something that made people want to help him.

It was a Friday afternoon, and everybody was at Link's except Jonas. Nobody in the building liked Jonas, so no one told him they were going to party at Link's. Jonas was fat and dark-skinned and always wore a quizzical smile that made people nervous.

As OD, who was temporarily staying at Link's, put it, you just never knew what the bastard was thinking.

OD was six-foot six and weighed three hundred pounds. His crown was bald, and the curly hair around the sides of his head—plus his tiny wire-rimmed glasses—made him look like something out of the nineteenth century.

Link could only get around in a wheelchair; he hadn't walked, even on crutches, for more than a year. He'd spent most of the past three years sitting in his apartment, drinking by himself, rehashing his life of injustices and loudly cursing the world until OD moved in. OD took Link out for a drive outside the city every Sunday and took him out to the bars every Friday night. OD and Link met when OD lived in one of the apartments upstairs with Bobbi, but after Bobbi threw him out, OD began hanging out at Link's and using Link's apartment as a base from which to harass Bobbi until she found another place to live. Link's place was too small for two people, but OD worked Sunday through Thursday nights as a meat cutter for a grocery store chain and slept on Link's couch all day. It worked out fine as far as Link was concerned; OD got free housing, and Link didn't have to live alone anymore. The only problem was that the landlord was after OD for breaking the lease he and Bobbi had signed, and OD had to play scarce whenever Landlord Larry came around, which was often.

The situation with the landlord was the main reason OD didn't like Jonas. Jonas, OD was sure, called Landlord Larry to let him know whenever OD was around. Everyone else in the building disliked Jonas for being Landlord Larry's stool-pigeon. So when Jonas showed up on Link's birthday, the room fell to silence. Even the stereo, which had been booming a Merle Haggard song about Oakies from Muskogee, went dead as the tape came to an end at about the same moment that Jonas appeared.

"Looks like a party," Jonas said with his small, weird smile. He leaned against the door frame in his smudged mechanic's overalls but did not come in.

"Don't let it fool you," Doris said. Doris lived in the apartment across the hall from Jonas. She was tall and red-headed and

was in nursing school at the university. She had told Link and
OD that she was sure it was Jonas who told Landlord Larry about
her cat. Pets were not allowed at The Hacienda.

"Goddam right it's a party," Link hollered from the couch,
where OD had set him. When Link was drunk, he hollered every sentence. "My fifty-second birthday!"

OD was the only one who didn't block his ears when Link
hollered. "It's not a party," OD said. "It's a meeting. Cost you
fifty bucks to join the club. And that's just to apply. Don't mean
we'll let you in."

Jonas reached for his wallet, thumbed through a wad of twen-
ties, and slapped the wallet shut. "I got the money but I'm not
sure I want to join the club."

OD and Doris might not have been happy to see Jonas at the
door, but Link didn't mind. He was glad to see anyone who
showed up. It was his birthday and he was drunk. Even with his
vision blurred, he could see the stubble on Jonas's grease-smeared
face. "You need to give up on that shaving cream and try na-
palm," he shouted. But he saw right away by the general silence
that he was not supposed to be friendly toward Jonas.

Link looked from OD to Doris to Evelyn, who was OD's
date. Evelyn was also Doris's classmate at nursing school and
lived in the building. She was short and stout, with hair cut short
in some places, left long in others. Her jaw sat atop her neck like
an iron. She'd been a secretary for ten years before she quit her
job to go back to school. Now Evelyn felt older and wiser than
just about everyone, including Link and OD.

"Just exactly what in the hell are you doing here?" Evelyn
asked Jonas.

"Just come to say hello." Jonas pulled a can of beer from the
paper sack he carried and handed it toward her.

"I just can't picture taking anything from you, Jonas. Least
of all anything I was planning to put near my mouth."

Jonas felt his little grin turn on. "How come you always try
to insult me?"

"I guess you just bring out the worst side of me."

Link noticed Jonas's beer bag, drained the can in his hand,
and burped loud and long. "I'll take one of those," Link hollered.
"It's my birthday. I'm fifty-two goddam years old, and I only
weigh a hundred and twenty."

Jonas crossed the floor to hand Link a beer, then stationed
himself again in the doorway. "Happy birthday," he said, raising

his can and smiling his dark smile.

"Thank you, Jonas. This ain't my brand, but I'll drink it any-way."

Only Jonas laughed.

The others silently watched Link drain the new can.

"I heard y'all were thinking about going out for something to eat," Jonas said.

"Where'd you hear that?" OD roared.

"I was leaning out my window a minute ago and heard you talking about it."

"Damn!" OD bellowed. "If there's anything I hate it's a thief, a liar and a fuckin' eavesdropper! I might just hate a eavesdropper worst of all."

OD stared at Jonas for a moment, then went to the stereo to put on a new tape. The attention shifted back to Link, who was opening his presents. Evelyn had given him some handkerchiefs.

"I know you get a lot of colds," she said. "I thought maybe you'd need these."

"Yeah," OD howled. "You ever see one of this guy's hand-kerchiefs? You have to beat it with a club to get it into the wash-ing machine."

In the ensuing laughter, which went on for several moments as OD acted out the pummeling of one of Link's handkerchiefs into submission, Jonas moved closer to Chad, who stood against the refrigerator.

"Where y'all gonna go eat?"

"I don't know, Jonas. You'll have to ask OD or Doris or somebody."

Chad stepped away, leaving Jonas alone. Jonas leaned against Link's kitchen counter and watched as OD turned the stereo way up and started dancing by himself. His massive feet shook the windows.

"Go man!" Link shouted.

More people arrived from upstairs—Edgar, the law student, and his roommate, Rawlins. They both had girls with them. Link began hollering again, and OD turned the stereo even higher.

"So are we going out for something to eat?" Edgar hollered to no one in particular.

"We haven't decided," Doris said, nodding slightly toward Jonas. When Edgar and his people saw Jonas, they nodded, too.

Jonas edged toward Link, who was unwrapping two cassette tapes. Link held one tape at arm's length, then brought it closer to his face, then held it a couple of feet away, shaking his head in frustration. Finally he handed it to Jonas.

"What the hell is this tape?"

"Willie Nelson," Jonas said. "Where do you think you're going to eat?"

Link fidgeted, and Jonas knew he would lie. "I dunno. Ask OD."

"You gonna tell OD about the other night?" Jonas asked.

Link's eyes picked up a different tape from his lap. "What's this one?"

"You gonna tell them about the other night? Especially OD."

"Jesus, Jonas...it'd kill OD to know what you did."

"Good."

The skin on Link's face seemed to sag with his pain. "Don't push it, Jonas. I'll tell him one of these days."

"I think he needs to know it today."

Link reached for Jonas's hand and looked as if he might cry. "It's my birthday, Man...don't make it hard for me."

Jonas yanked free from Link's heartfelt grasp and lightly brushed the freed hand through Link's hair. Doris had come up beside him to hand Link another present.

"Mind if I come with you guys?" Jonas asked her.

"You'll have to ask Link," she said. "It's *his* party."

"Hell it is. It's OD's party."

"Why would you want to go when you know nobody here can stand you?" she asked, finally looking at him.

"I'm kind of conducting a poll."

"What, to see how many people in one room can't stand you?"

"Yeah. Something like that. And to see what else I can do to piss everybody off." Jonas smiled. "You got pretty hair, though; I'll give you that. I like how it goes every whichaway."

Doris shuddered and backed away. "I don't want you giving me *nothing*."

"So, can I come or not?"

Doris shrugged. "Do I look like a travel agent? Ask Link."

"Link, can I come with you guys?" Jonas asked, raising his voice enough for everyone to hear.

Link squirmed and glanced toward OD. "I dunno...ask OD."

"Don't give me that crap," OD yelled. "Why does he have to ask me?"

"Well..." Link looked from face to face, then took a swig of his beer.

"How about it, OD?" Jonas asked.

"You gonna put it on me anyway?" OD said to Link. He turned in his chair and faced Jonas. "In that case...no. You can't come with us. Okay?"

"Oh hell," Link said. "Let him come."

OD's voice exploded. "Then why in hell are you telling him to ask me?"

"Because the whole thing was your idea," Link yelled back

"I think we should take a vote," Doris said. "My vote is no. Not after he turned my cat in to Landlord Larry. And I had to have the damn thing *put away*. Thirty bucks plus I lost my little cat."

No one else voted. The silence lasted only a moment, then a new song started, and Link looked at the stereo speakers and smiled. "That's my song," he bellowed. "Bad, Bad Leroy Brown,' with Mr. Sinatra on the chords. Sing it, baby."

OD and Evelyn started dancing and whooping again.

Jonas leaned against the opposite door frame and watched everyone. He finished his beer and stuffed the empty can in his sack. Then he set the sack on the counter and backed out the door. He needed to use the bathroom, and the only place he knew he could feel comfortable was in his own apartment.

*****

Link and OD and the crowd had been at The Corral over an hour when Jonas showed up. The Corral was one of the few places other than the chains where you could get food all night, and the specialty was ribs, either beef or pork. The restaurant was a hodge-podge of rooms that had been added on to the main part of the place, which was a ninety-seat dining room. The paneled walls were covered with Bear Bryant and Shug Jordan posters. Link assumed that Link's crowd would be in the back room, which OD liked to call The OD Parker Memorial Dining Room. He'd even autographed one wall with three-foot-high strokes of a paintbrush.

Jonas approached the door of the room but did not immediately come in.

OD was the first to spot Jonas and whispered, "Who the hell told him we were coming here?"

"Not I," Doris said.

"Don't look at me," said Evelyn.

"Must have been you."

OD grimaced and held his stomach. "I wouldn't tell Jonas

Dillard where to find the nearest hydrant if he needed to piss."

"Hey you guys," Jonas said. No one looked at him or spoke to him.

"I guess I missed the bus when y'all left."

The chatter had died the moment Jonas walked in.

"Some people just don't know when they're not invited," OD said. "Personally, I can't stand that in people. When I want to have someone come somewhere with me, I tell them so. If I don't want them, I don't say nothing."

Jonas stared around the long table, waiting for someone to look at him just for a second. Link was the one who finally looked up. Jonas could see that Link was between the old rock and the hard place, wanting to let Jonas join them but afraid he'd irritate the others if he did.

"Saw your sign on your door," Jonas said. "*Gone with wind— Be back soon.* Cute. But it shoulda said, *Gone with windbag.*"

Jonas shook his head. "Don't you think I figured out a long time ago that particular sign means The Co-ral?"

OD raised his finger toward Jonas and cocked his head to the side. "Have I ever told you that smile of yours and the way you shake your head like you smarter than everybody else gets up my ass? Sideways?"

OD and Jonas continued to stare at each other and finally OD looked at his ribs, picked one up in a way that Jonas thought almost delicate, and started gnawing again.

"Are you going to sit down?" Link asked.

He had only beer bottles on the table in front of him, no food.

"I don't think so."

"Good," OD said without looking up.

"Jonas is my friend," Link said absently, quietly.

"You're drunk," OD said. "Most of the time you enjoy running Jonas down just as much as the rest of us do."

"Well, I'm moving out," Jonas said. "You can run me down all you want to after I leave. At least I won't have to listen. Not that it ever bothered me the damnedest bit, considering the source."

"If you wouldn't eavesdrop, you wouldn't have to hear it."

The waitress came in with more beers, and Link watched her long, quick fingers pass the bottles around the table.

"It's my birthday," Link said, smiling up at her.

"Happy *birthday*, sweetheart," the waitress said. She was tall and thin and had bleached streaks in her long, black hair. She wore a bikini top with hotpants and fishnet stockings and red spike heels. She came around to Link's side of the table and kissed him fully on the lips.

"All right," OD shouted. "*Get it on!*"

Everyone at the table laughed and clapped, and Link's face flushed deep red as the waitress kissed him again, pressing a breast against his shoulder a moment before she gathered the empty bottles and scurried away.

Link wore his biggest smile of the night. "She's byoooootiful, Man...."

Jonas picked up an empty chair near the door and carried it toward Link's end of the table. "Maybe I will sit down a minute after all. If I can sit next to the guest of honor here...happy birthday, Link."

Link looked at him suspiciously, as if he knew exactly why Jonas wanted to sit so close to him. Jonas set his chair close enough to touch Link's. He sat down and leaned to whisper in Link's ear.

"Sorry you weren't willing to tell them about how I dragged you and OD out of the apartment and called the fire department before the whole place went up."

Link didn't whisper, he only muttered. "Jonas...goddam it!"

"Uh oh, it's tell me a secret time," OD said, leaning an inch closer to the whispering.

"I don't mind saving *your* life," Jonas went on into Link's ear. "I just wanted that fat fuck beside you to know he owes me for saving *his*."

Link sat back in his chair and looked for a long moment at Jonas. "What the hell difference does it make?"

"It makes a big difference." But even as he said it, Jonas saw that Link was right; the whole thing made no difference whatsoever. It was one of Link's famous moments of inebriated lucidity. He could hardly hold his head up.

Jonas sighed. "So what does he think happened?"

"The firemen dragged him out."

Jonas shook his head at Link and felt his smile spread almost painfully. When he spoke again, he didn't bother to whisper.

"I guess that makes sense. Makes perfect sense. Anybody would think that."

Now it was Link who whispered. "He thinks it because that's what I told him."

Jonas tried to make his smile relax before he got a cramp in his facial muscles. As he glanced around the table, he was pleased to see the others talking about the ribs and the baked beans and the waitress's bad hair-streaking job instead of sneering their silence his way. He stood up and held his hand toward Link.

"Anyway...take care of yourself. Don't be cooking any more bacon fat when you're too drunk to pay attention. And the only other person in the room is out cold."

Link grabbed the hand, a little too earnestly, as always, and pumped it slowly up and down as he listened to Jonas.

"...And use them new handkerchiefs instead of just blowing your nose in the sink," Jonas said. He laughed, yanked his hand away, and tousled Link's hair. "And don't forget to say your prayers!"

The silence descended once again as they watched Jonas leave. Link weaved in his chair, studying the bottle in his hand.

"Thank *God* he's gone," Doris said, turning her eyes toward the ceiling.

"Amen," said Chad.

Link looked up from his bottle toward the wavering faces seated around the table.

"Jonas wasn't a bad guy," Link droned. "He was the only one in that whole building that came downstairs and helped me move in...."

"He was a pain in the ass," OD said with a single tap of his bottle against the table.

"And a snake, and a liar, and a filthy, smelly sum-bitch."

Link suddenly swarmed with hatred for OD. He studied his friend's rounded face, small lenses that somehow shrank his eyes, the curly wisps along the sides of his head, the delight on his lips.

"You don't know it, but Jonas pulled your ass out of that fire!"

OD's burst of laughter was so loud it hurt even Link's ears. "Is that the story he told you? And you believed him?"

"I was there. I saw it."

"You're drunk," OD said. "Let's get that waitress back in here so's we can order you some take-out. Then we'll go back home."

Sign Language

The first time I went to Canada was at night. Gene says, let's go to Montreal, so we took a left and headed north. I said I thought it was getting kind of late, and Gene said Montreal was just a couple of hours away. I asked him if he'd ever been there and he said no, but that almost everybody he knew had been, and they all said Montreal was just a couple of hours up the road.

Now that we were headed north, I started wondering if there was a map in the glove compartment. Gene said no and asked me to hand him another beer. I figured as long as we were headed north, we were basically on the right path. I started thinking of the Canadians who used to come down to Portland every summer, and how they'd play golf at this course I caddied at. It was the only public course where the out-of-staters could play, since all the other courses were private clubs. I usually caddied for one of the regular local guys on the weekend, but during the week, the only people playing were the out-of-staters, and a lot of them were Canadians. I hated caddying for the Canucks. You never knew what they were saying, and I didn't know what I was supposed to say to them. Every time I opened my mouth they'd just go, "Huh? Huh?" So I gave up finally. I told Hamilton, the caddy master, that I wasn't caddying for any more Canucks. He told me I'd damned well better caddy for a Canuck any time he told me to.

The next time I got a Canuck bag, I just kept my mouth shut and kind of communicated in sign language. The Canuck was one of those short ones (most of them are) with bushy black hair and a little skinny moustache that was like a pencil line over his lip. His jaw muscles twitched all the time. I didn't try to talk to him, and I got the idea he liked that because he didn't try to talk to me, either. When he didn't know what club to use, he just shrugged and I'd give him a club. His game was easy to figure out, so I clubbed him pretty good. Let's put it this way: when he made a bad shot, it was because he made a bad shot and not because I gave him the wrong club. He shot better than anybody in the foursome that day, and Tommy Jacques, who was one of the caddies who spoke French, told me the guy was really pleased and that he wanted me to caddy for him every day. They were there for two weeks. It got so he knew what I was thinking and I knew what he was thinking, and we never had to say a single word.

I never saw him crack a grin except once. We were waiting for this threesome of women ahead of us to tee off. Two of them were hags, but the other one was young, maybe twenty-one or two. When she bent over to tee up her ball, you could see right down her blouse, and her jugs just about fell out. The Canuck looked at me, I looked at him, and we both smiled for a second. That was the only time.

He was a cheap bastard, though. He never gave me a tip or bought me a soda the whole two weeks I caddied for him. The Canucks all had booze in their golf bags, and I nipped pretty regular, knowing it was as close to a tip as I was going to get.

"Why ain't you drinking?" Gene asked.

"I just opened it. What do you care? You got a map anywhere?"

"Hell no. What do you want a map for?"

"Make sure we're on the right road for Montreal."

"Don't sweat it." Gene drained his can and tossed it onto the back seat. "Crack me another, will ya?"

Gene always came across as pushy, but once you got used to it, he didn't bother you much. He was real lanky and looked kind of underfed. He had high cheekbones and little tiny slits of eyes that gave him a mean look. He was pretty tough on the football field, always looking to take down guys who were twice his size. The only time I ever saw him admit to any kind of pain was while we were getting our tattoos. Gene turned white, and I thought he was going to pass out. He actually made the tattoo guy stop in the middle, and to this day he has half a heart tattooed on his arm. He tells everybody he ordered it special like that, and that he's going to get half of an ass tattooed on his other arm. He couldn't take it, that tattoo pain.

I opened him another can and watched him guzzle half of it

and then slip the can between his legs. "Ahhh...look at them mountains. Wouldn't you like to own a mansion on top of one of those babies?"

"I don't want to own a mansion," I told him. "I want to own a mountain."

Gene and I worked together at the rubber factory in Dover. It wasn't really a rubber factory at all; it was a *plastics* factory that made stuff that *used to* be made of rubber. We made stuff for cars—dashboard covers, console covers, stuff like that. Even though it was plastic, everybody in Dover still called it the rubber factory. Once you worked there, that's all you could smell, no matter where you were or what you were doing. That smell just followed you everywhere. I mean, if you walked into a bar, you knew which guys worked at the rubber factory. And we'd all say something like, "Goddam, man...you stink!" It was just a way to say hello.

I started watching the houses and stuff along the road. It was mostly dairy farms with these rolling pastures and barns and silos and old pickups in the dooryards. I got to wondering what it must be like to work on a farm, up at dawn and busting your ass until sundown. Every farmer I ever knew smelled like cow dung, even when he dressed up for church on Sunday. That got me thinking about the factory again and wondering how long after I quit working there I'd still smell like burning plastic. Before I went to work in the rubber factory I had a job as a house painter and I always smelled like either paint or turpentine.

Next thing I knew we were smelling something *real* bad.

"Good God!" Gene says.

"I bet it's a paper mill. Berlin's got a bunch of mills. Whew...awful, huh? Worse than the damn rubber factory." I got this urge to roll down the window and get a strong blast of the God-awful smell. Just about then we came over a rise and there was the town of Berlin below us with smoke spouting from big stacks. It was funny how you could see the smoke plain as day even when it was almost dark out.

"God-*damn*...roll that window up!"

"Don't you want a good whiff?"

"No. Roll it up. It's making my beer taste bad."

I rolled the window up, but the car was full of the smell now. The warm air from the heater made it worse.

"Think it's bad as the rubber factory?"

Gene shuddered. "God, yes. Worse."

"Think we'll be working there in thirty years? Like old Hammond?"

"Hell, no," Gene said.

"What are *you* going to do?"

"Probably start my own business..."

"What kind of business?"

"I got a few ideas. I sure as hell ain't working at Rubbex forever."

I could tell he was starting to get pissed. I waited for him to come up with some idea for a business but he didn't. I couldn't leave him alone at that point and just kept toying with him.

"Yeah...I can see you joining the bowling league and winning a plaque. That's what's going to happen to you. Win a fuckin' plaque for bowling."

"Like hell."

"Josephine will get fat and cut her hair short and stop using deodorant, and you won't even care. That is, if she really is stupid enough to marry you."

"Shut up, Wes."

"You'll have some old klunker of a car, just the way old Hammond does, because he still doesn't make enough to live on." I was tempted to really get him going about Josephine, but the whole thing with Josephine just depressed me.

"Wake me up when we get to Canada," I told him, and I slouched down in my seat and pulled the visor of my hat over my eyes. After a second, I turned the radio on. It just made static, but I wanted it on. I knew the static would make me sleepy after awhile.

I guess I slept. It was more like daydreaming, but time went by faster than it does when you're awake, so I guess I was sleeping at least part of the time. I kept thinking about how Gene had really gotten the best of me the last time we got in a fight. I used to kill him on a regular basis when we were in high school. We were both on the boxing and wrestling teams. It got me thinking that I was really on some kind of decline—only twenty-one and already too old to fight worth a damn, too fat to get girls, too stupid with my money to ever get anything saved so I could get out of Dover. It's funny how just changing towns can change your whole personality and outlook. In Portland, Gene and I were really close friends. But in Dover, all that changed. While he was staying with me, before he got his own place, everything he did got on my nerves—the way he left a mess everywhere, the way he always finished anything that was left in the fridge, like the last beer, the last can of spaghetti sauce, the last doughnut. And the way he treated Josephine. He met her through me and then proceeded to just move in on her. The main reason we were still friends was because neither one of us had met that many new people in Dover. He and Josephine had their ups and downs from the beginning, and whenever they were having a down, Gene would start dropping by my place, drinking my beer and never bringing any with him. That kind of cramped my style because whenever Gene and Josephine were on the outs, she wanted to come around and get a little from me.

Rumor had it he'd knocked her up and didn't want to marry her. I kept waiting for him to say something about it, but he never did. And I didn't ask because I didn't want to hear what he might say.

*****

I woke up when he turned the static off.

"What's the matter?"

"Driving me nuts," he said. "Been on two friggin' hours."

"We in Canada yet?"

"No."

"Thought you said it was just a couple hours up the road?"

"It's a little farther. Don't sweat it."

"You stop for directions or something?"

"No. There was a sign back a few miles that said the border was up this way a bit. Go back to sleep."

"What time is it?"

"Eight, nine. I dunno. Don't sweat it...we'll get there."

I closed my eyes again, but I had the feeling I wasn't going to sleep anymore. And I didn't. Next thing I knew I was thinking about Josephine. Josephine was not only not a virgin, she'd slept with half the guys in Dover, Portsmouth and even a few of the college boys over in Durham. But she was gorgeous in her own way. She was a little out of proportion, with wide hips and thick legs and small breasts and a skinny little neck. Her face was absolutely beautiful, and if you could have stuck it on a better body, she would have been Miss America. She was blond and wore her hair in a pony tail, but a lot of hair always got out of the rubber band and just kind of fell around her face. The way she talked to you was the best part, kind of in a whisper, looking around every now and then, like everything was a conspiracy. She'd touch my arm and lean a little closer so I could smell her breath, which was like apples or something. Real clean.

I couldn't see her with Gene. *He* claimed they were engaged, but she didn't have a ring, and there wasn't anything in the newspaper about it. Not that it has to be in the paper, but just the way Gene was going about the whole thing seemed kind of second class to me. I never thought of myself as being old-fashioned, but maybe I am, in a way. It's not that I doubted that he was in love with her because I knew from my own experience that it was hard to know her without being in love with her, but it just seemed to me like he didn't really understand how incredible she was. I mean, he did, but he didn't. She had more feeling than anybody I ever knew for people who had it rough, especially little kids. She was always taking kids in her neighbourhood to the movies or to the swimming pool at the park. I was thinking about the rotten life she was going to have with Gene when his voice came galloping at me out of the silence in my head.

"Here's Canada."

I sat up in my seat. Sure enough, there was a great big sign that said, *Quebec, the Beautiful Province*, and a bunch of gobbledeegook in French. We had to stop at this little booth, and these two funny looking little French guys in uniforms came out and started asking questions in their stupid accents. One of them circled the car about three times. He seemed to be checking out the tires. I got a kick out of the questions they were asking, like what country we were citizens of. When the guy asked me where I was born, I got that feeling like I used to have at the golf course and started stammering. The guard looked at me kind of weird, which made it even worse. I couldn't say a damned thing. Then the two guards were staring at me and jabbering at each other.

"He's from New Hampshire, too," Gene said.

"How long you be in Canada?"

"Dunno."

The guards looked at each other again. "You must tell us a time how long you would be in Canada."

Gene shrugged. "Dunno."

"Two days? Two weeks?"

"Naw. Just a little while," Gene said.

One guard shook his clipboard at us. "Two days?"

"Naw, we gotta be back at work Monday."

"One day?"

"Yeah, that's about right."

I was glad Gene was doing the talking because I felt like I had a baseball in my throat. Just before we pulled away from the guard booth, one of the guards asked me if I was sick. I shook my head no, but I didn't think he believed me. In fact, I'm sure they thought I was nuts.

Gene pulled off slowly, watching his mirror. "What the hell's the matter with you?"

"Nothing. It's weird. I think I'm allergic to Canadians."

I noticed some road signs, and my throat tightened up again. Everything was in French. I started wondering how in hell we were going to get where we were going, but then we saw a sign.

"Shit...Montreal's a hundred miles...."

"Don't sweat it," Gene said. "We got all night."

I sat back and tried to relax, but that uneasy feeling stayed with me. I felt like I was definitely in a place where I didn't belong. The more I tried to figure out why I felt that way, the weirder I felt.

*****

Canada was different, all right. For one thing, the smell of cow manure was just about everywhere, and once it got inside that car, there wasn't much we could do about it. The road was bumpier than it was on the States side, and the night seemed darker, not to mention colder. I remembered seeing a map of Canada one time. The damned place goes all the way up to the North Pole.

I reached for a beer to try to wake up a little more, but there wasn't any. Gene had polished off the six-pack while I was asleep. That meant he'd had five of them and I'd had one. Plus, he'd had three before we even decided to go to Canada and stopped to get a fresh six for the trip.

"This your first time in a foreign country?" Gene asked.

"Yeah. How about you?"

"Yeah. Funny place, huh?"

"That's for shit sure. I like America better."

"Me too."

The road was getting wider, I saw more and more houses, so I figured we were coming to some town. I was right. It was a funny little place, and the houses were real close to the road. No sidewalk. Wouldn't want to raise cats there, let alone a kid. When I saw a little grocery store, I told Gene to pull over.

"Want to split another six-pack?" I asked him.

"No, I guess not."

I was hoping he would because I didn't want to have to go into the store and ask for it myself. "C'mon, one more...."

"Naw. I don't want to fall asleep."

"Well, go in and get *me* one, will you?"

"Get it yourself."

"Thanks a lot. Prick."

I got out and crossed the little parking lot. My hands started shaking the second I was inside the store. The clerk looked up from his newspaper and jabbered something to me. I just nodded. He was fat and bald on top and wore this white apron that was all smeared with what looked like pickle juice. I looked around the store for a beer cooler and didn't see one. He jabbered again, and I figured he was asking me what I wanted. I held my hand like I was holding a beer can and then tipped my head back and made believe I was drinking. The clerk's face lit up, and he went right to a cooler and pulled out a bottle of Coke. I shook my head no. He tried a bottle of orange juice and I shook my head again. I made the drinking motion again and took a few staggering steps and looked back at him with what I hoped was a real stupid grin. He flashed a big smile and went to another cooler, one that had the beer. I nodded. He nodded. For a second I wished there were some titties right there for us to smirk at each other about.

He went back to the counter and wrote the price on a pad of paper. It seemed kind of high, but I paid it anyway. As I was walking out the door, I noticed a clock that said ten. Damn, and we weren't even there yet. I wondered, for the first time, really, why the hell we'd decided to go to Canada in the first place.

Gene was sitting in the car with the engine running. It was damned cold in Canada. I turned the heater on full blast for a few minutes and cracked a beer. The road turned into a four-lane, and the next sign for Montreal said sixty miles. Let me tell you, those Canadians drive like they're all training to be test pilots or something. Gene had the old Plymouth cranked up to seventy-five, and the Canucks were passing us like we were in a funeral procession. I wasn't sure the Plymouth would hold up to speeds like that. It used to be my car, but I sold it to Gene one afternoon when I needed money. The tires were bad, I didn't much trust the brakes, and the mirrors, including the inside one, were all cracked, so you couldn't see shit behind you.

"Slow down. Town's gonna be shut down by the time we get there," I said. "So there's no hurry. You wanna just go back?" I figured we'd already seen Canada, and there wasn't much sense to going on.

"They say Montreal's quite a place," Gene said. "We come this far. Might as well go the rest of the way." After a minute he says, "I heard they got a lot of work in Montreal."

It all came to me then. I knew just what he was doing. He really did have Josephine knocked up, and he was planning to just stay in Montreal and let her figure out for herself what she was going to do with the kid.

"You planning to stay?"

He didn't look at me. "I dunno. Maybe. Depends."

"On what?"

"What it's like. Might be a good place to start a business...."

"Thought you were engaged?"

Gene just smiled and pointed to a sign: Montreal ten miles. "Hope everything isn't already shut down," he said.

The place didn't *look* shut down, even at midnight. The road had about fifty lanes and was packed with cars that were all screaming by and honking at each other. One car had this girl that looked like Josephine. I decided to start looking for a better job when I got home so that when I called her with the news about Gene staying in Montreal, I could tell her I was getting out of the rubber factory and had a decent future looking at me.

"Look at that bridge," Gene said.

Everything started to throb and my eyes got blurred as we started up this big ramp, cars flying by us in six lanes. The whole city was lighted up, and it was huge. Biggest place I'd ever seen, spread out everywhere and lights blinking and big tall neon signs zipping by you and everybody honking at each other. Montreal was some place all right. There was a big river under the bridge, and I could see these huge ships tied at the docks—much bigger than anything I'd ever seen in the harbor at Portsmouth. And more and more cars flooding by.

"I told you it wouldn't be shut down," Gene said.

"I guess not. Well...we've seen Montreal. Want to head back?"

"Hell no. Don't you want to have a beer or something?"

"I got one right here."

"I notice you didn't offer me one," he said.

"You drank that last six-pack, Asshole. Besides, I did offer you one."

"Not since we got to Montreal."

I yanked one out of the bag. "Here."

He popped his can open and took a long swig, still watching me, trying to get my goat by not watching the road. I knew damned well he was planning to stay in Montreal. That was fine by me. I'd just take a bus back to Dover. He could stay in Montreal for ten years for all I cared.

"Where do you think we get off?" he asked. "There a Main Street?"

"Dunno."

"What would that be in French, Main Street?"

"Don't ask me. I don't know a friggin' word of French. I don't know how in hell these Canadians get through life talking a language like that."

I was feeling good, thinking how I'd be on a bus back to Dover with something going on in my life for a change. The kid might not be Gene's at all, for that matter....

"I'm getting off here," he said.

We slid down this long, curving exit ramp. There were tall buildings all around, so I knew we were downtown. Here it was after midnight, and the streets were crawling with people—a zillion cars with horns honking, lights flashing, the whole business.

"There's a bar. Let's park."

Gene pulled around a corner into a little street and pulled up beside a sign that probably said *no parking*. I noticed that they painted the curb yellow in no parking zones, just the way they do it at home. I was glad to see they did at least one thing right.

The bar was one of those old-fashioned looking places with high ceilings and fans hanging down and a long bar with all these seedy looking French guys standing along it. I mean, they were still wearing duck-tail haircuts and tight, shiny bell-bottom pants and pointy shoes, even in the nineties. I noticed nobody was talking, and they all started staring at me and Gene. I like being stared at by a bunch of people I don't know kind of like I love spoiled milk. There were all these little puddles all over the floor like someone spilled beer while they were taking a leak. Gene ordered us two beers, and the bartender understood him. I was amazed at the way he could just say whatever he wanted to and the Canadians understood exactly what he was saying.

*****

We found a table and waited for the beers. "There's something I wanted to talk to you about," Gene said, smiling with all this importance. "Which is why I brought you all the way here to Montreal."

I had to smile, and I think he understood for a second how much I despised him.

"Goddamn it, man," he said, "we're in a foreign country. We never been to one. Don't it make you feel like you done something for once in your life?"

I realized that when we got back to the rubber factory, Gene—if he ever came back, which he might never do—would be telling everybody for weeks about his big trip to a foreign country and all the hotshot things he did there, even though his so-called foreign country wasn't any farther away than Massachusetts. I'd be coming on the shift after him, and the second-shift guys that were still there would ask me every night about something Gene would have told them about the great Montreal.

"I don't have to go to a foreign friggin' country to feel good."

Gene drew back and looked at me seriously for a minute. "Is that what's eating you? You're afraid you're going to get stuck at the rubber factory for the rest of your life? Shit, Man, don't worry about that. You can come work for me after I get set up in business for myself."

That cracked me up. Here was Gene, a guy I put up and found a job for, and he's telling me he's gonna give me a job in his business. It was more than I could take.

"I'll be waiting for the big call."

"Could be in the next month or two," he said, all serious again.

"Oh. Got some hot lead, huh?"

"Yeah...as a matter of fact, I do."

"Tell me about it."

"Well...it's part of what I wanted to talk to you about." He smiled again. "That's why we're having this little conference here in Montreal. Josephine's old man offered me the bread to take over a shoe repair shop. I'm not really sold yet on the shoe business idea, but it could go somewhere I guess...."

"What the hell you know about shoes?"

"Nothing. Don't have to. Place already has an old guy working there who knows *everything* there is about fixing shoes. I mean, he could turn a fuckin' tin can into a shoe. All I have to do is kind of hang around, pay the old man a few bucks, and take home the rest. Sounds decent, huh?"

"Sounds pretty risky to me."

Gene shrugged. "Only risky part is Josephine. Never been sure I can trust her."

"I didn't know you and Josephine's father were that close."

"Well...when you're going to marry somebody's daughter, you get to talking to them." Gene looked up at me with this weird little grin. "I'll tell you a secret. I know for a fact that you didn't get Josephine because her old man didn't like you."

I knew that. I didn't much care for him, either. I thought he was one of these strict old tyrants who never gave Josephine credit for anything, and that was basically why she went hog-wild and slept around once she got a little bit of freedom.

I'd forgotten for a moment that Gene was even there until he started laughing. "You know what he said to Josephine? He said you didn't have any ambition. That's why he likes me, because I *do*."

I watched him start running his finger around and around in the grime on the table. I wanted to tear him apart right then, but I didn't want to end up in jail in a foreign country. I started wondering what else Josephine had told him about me. Like, I wondered if she told him about the night at the park. That was the first time I actually tried to make it with Josephine. The whole thing was a disaster. I mean, nothing happened. There we were, both naked, both wanting it real bad, and I couldn't do a damn thing. Instead of getting bigger, it just got smaller, like somebody had tossed the ocean on it in the middle of winter. She didn't complain or nothing, but she always treated me different after that. It wasn't long before Gene came along. That's when it started getting good with Josephine and me—when she'd sneak over to see me after she and Gene had a row. "I can piss him off anytime I want to," she told me once as we lay together in the candlelight (she'd brought the candle) at the Holiday Inn in Portsmouth. "And then you and I can get together...."

Gene was still smiling. "Yeah. I know all about you. Anyway, what I wanted to ask you here in Montreal is if you'd be my best man."

I was the one that started laughing then. I'm not sure why. Maybe it seemed like the safest thing to do. Or maybe I was laughing because I'd read the whole situation so completely wrong. Laughing was my way of kicking myself in the ass. I decided right then and there that come Friday payday, I was leaving Dover and never coming back. Worst town I ever saw, with all those rotten, stinking little factories. I knew one thing: I wasn't about to be best man to a guy whose girlfriend I was boinking. And had just boinked a few nights before. And might *keep* boinking even after she was married.

"I'll have to think about that," I said.

Gene's face got all twisted up with surprise and he stared at me until the beers finally came. I guzzled mine down in one long swig. I'd already drunk about ten that day, starting around noon, but guzzling that one Canadian beer gave me a whole new buzz. I knew the Plymouth was on empty, and that I was holding all the cash we had between us, except for a dollar or two.

"Order me another one," I said. I got up and went to the men's room, took a piss, then asked the first person I saw where the bus terminal was. He told me to go two blocks down this way, and five blocks down that way, and I'd see it right in front of me. I mean, he just spit it out and didn't have an accent or nothing. It came to me right then that all those Canadians really do speak English and just pretend they don't.

The Cookie Trick

I was tired as hell by nine o'clock and didn't need Bainard
and his carload of idiots pulling in at The Winning Wheel drive-
in, flashing their lights and catcalling at me while I was waiting
on the other cars. Plus, I'd just spilled a milkshake down this
one guy's new car.

I had a tray that had a broken hook. I just hung the tray on
the guy's window and figured everything was okay. The next
thing I know, the milkshake goes splat on the ground and the
guy yells, hey! I look back, and there's milkshake all down the
door and all over the pavement. So Old Man Crandall, the owner,
was already pretty irked at me.

Then Bainard and the rest of them pull in. It was their night
off. Bainard was supposed to be working instead of me, but we
decided to switch nights off so he could study for his shop test.
But here he was out cruising, driving the others around like he
was their chauffeur. They were drinking, too. I know Savard and
Curran were. They had a bag on the floor in the backseat and
they had Jumbo Julie with them. Curran and Savard were feeling her up there in the back seat, and she kept squealing and
telling them to cut it out. But you could tell she loved it. Jumbo
Julie's a good kid—much more of a buddy than a girlfriend. She's
pretty stout, to use a polite word, but she has a pretty face and
real pretty black hair. She grabbed Savard's hat and put it on—
this straw thing he won throwing darts at balloons down at Old
Orchard Beach. Savard grabbed it back and whacked her shoulder hard. Savard gets real touchy about his hat. The way he wore
it pulled down over his eyes made him look kind of like a thug
on a Caribbean vacation.

Curran just sat there with his goofy smile. He was the pimply member of the crew. He hardly ever talked, just smiled. And

then Bainard, with his smart mouth and baseball cap turned backward. All three guys were goofballs. Julie, who was actually pretty smart, hung out with them just to have friends.

I knew Cramps—that's what we called Old Man Crandall—was watching and didn't much like the fact that I was talking to those clowns. But we had only two other cars, and they already had their food. Funny how Cramps didn't mind how much anybody goofed off when there were lots of cars, but when it was slow, he'd get a hair up his ass over nothing. Course, he already had about fifty hairs there because of the milkshake thing.

Jumbo Julie wanted a Coke. Nobody else wanted anything, including Bainard, which is what made me pretty sure he was drinking. I got irked thinking about it because the car was half mine, and I knew how Bainard drove when he was drunk. I knew it wouldn't do any good to say anything to him about it right then. He'd just call me *Old Lady*. That would get Savard and Curran going, and the whole carload of them would be calling me *Old Lady*. That's what they called me at school. Frankly, I was kinda surprised they were carrying on like that in front of Cramps. I could see him looking out of his little window where he put the orders out for us to pick up. He had these eyebrows that were huge and always mussed-up looking, like with one point of hairs going one way and another point going another. He'd lower his head and glare at people with his mussed-up eyebrows. No clue how ridiculous he looked.

I never let the old bastard bother me. I mean, I didn't go out of my way to get his goat, but I didn't whimper at him either when he'd get the rag on. Now Savard, he'd go out of his way to annoy Cramps. Nothing made Savard happier than pissing the old man off and getting the rest of us blamed. Savard's favorite time to get Cramps going about some little thing—punching holes in the paper cups, or squeezing ketchup on a bundle of paper napkins—was just when he was getting off the afternoon shift and we were coming on for the night. Then Savard would leave, and the rest of us would have to put up with old Cramps.

Cramps particularly loved to ride me. He hated anyone who was smart, and when the others told him that I got straight A's, he started hating me right away. Gave me the garbage detail and made me clean out the grease trap twice in one week. He hated all of us, but he always seemed to hate me the most. And we weren't exactly nuts about Cramps. The only reason we worked there was because it was hard for high school kids to find a job in the coastal towns any time but the summer. That's why we put up with him. And Cramps hated training new people, so I guess that's why he put up with us.

I was surprised that Cramps wasn't trying to run Bainard and the other guys off that night. Like I said, he got antsy when business was slow. He just leaned out his little window where we picked up our orders and glared, but he didn't say anything. It was warmer than usual, and a moth flitted under the dirty yellow bulb that hung over Cramps's window. Cramps didn't seem to notice.

He pulled himself back inside when an old Chrysler came in. The Chrysler hardly made a sound when it pulled up to the dock, two spaces away from Bainard's Olds. Bainard and *my* Olds, that is. There was a guy and a girl inside. They looked older than us; maybe college kids. I thought I'd seen them come in the previous Saturday night, but I couldn't say for sure.

"Help you?"

The guy had a shaved head and a little gold hoop in his ear lobe and a nasty little smile under his mustache. He wasn't drunk or anything, but he had this nasty look. It made me kind of uneasy.

Bainard and the others quieted down and just stared at the newcomers. They all cut their eyes away when the guy in the Chrysler looked over at them.

The girl was the opposite of the guy. She was absolutely gorgeous—long, blond hair, nice titties, just a tiny bit of lipstick. She wore a little pink blouse, white shorts, red sneakers. She was laughing over something and kept slapping the guy's arm. I asked them what they wanted to order. He wanted four hamburgers with everything. She just wanted some fried clams. They both ordered Cokes.

I went and hollered the order in to Cramps. He already had the hamburger patties on the griddle. I started fixing a tray. Napkins, toothpicks, and two packages of cookies. It was the cookies that started the trouble.

The cookies weren't free, but we couldn't tell people that. We were supposed to put a package of cookies on every tray. If the customers ate them, we'd charge them for the cookies. If they didn't eat them, we'd just bring them back. People who came there all the time knew about it, but every night we'd get at least one car that didn't know about the cookie trick, and they'd eat the cookies, then get real ticked when we charged them extra.

I hated it. Talk about being embarrassed. It was the worst thing about working at The Winning Wheel. The other guys didn't like it, either, except Savard. He loved the cookie trick. He'd come away from collecting from a car that didn't know about the cookie trick and he'd be laughing. He'd go over by the window and tell Cramps how surprised they were. Cramps never thought Savard was funny. In fact, Cramps took the cookie trick very seriously. He claimed that the cookie money was his retirement fund.

Anyway, I brought the tray with the cookies on it over to the black Chrysler. The guy was still looking mean, but at least he was looking mean at his food and not at me. His girl had her legs tucked up under her on the seat. I hadn't noticed them making out or anything, so I couldn't tell how much she liked him. I had to tell him to roll his window up a little so I could hang the tray on it. Then I went back and stood by the window to wait until they were done eating.

Cramps glanced at Bainard and Curran and them. "Whadda them fools want?"

"A Coke."

"You go out there and tell them they'd better order something more than a Coke or they're gonna hafta shove off."

I went back out to the car. "What else you want?"

Savard's hand came out of the back window and tried to hit me in the nuts.

Jumbo Julie laughed. "I'm hungry. Buy me something," she told Savard.

"Buy you something? Hah! You oughta go on a diet."

She turned around to Curran. "Buy me something?"

"I ain't got any money. You buy *me* something?"

"Cramps says you gotta go if you don't buy more than one Coke," I said.

They all looked at me like I was on his side and not theirs.

"Okay," Bainard says. "Bring us two Cokes."

I didn't say anything else. I just went back and ordered another Coke. Cramps raised the screen and leaned out the window. I could see he was on the verge of hollering at them before he remembered we had other customers. He pulled himself back in and lowered the screen.

"Tell them it's two bucks per if all they want is two Cokes."

I went back and told them. They all looked up at the window to see if Cramps was watching, and when they saw he wasn't, they laughed.

"Okay. Bring me a Coke, too," Savard said.

"You got the money?" I asked.

He waved his hand and said, "Sure, sure; don't worry about it, Grandma."

I went back and got Savard's Coke. Cramps didn't say anything, so I figured that three Cokes was good enough for him. When I brought the Coke to the car, Savard grabbed it, took a sip, and handed it back to me.

"It ain't fizzy enough," he says.

"Take it back. I ain't paying for it."

I figured Cramps would come out and run them off. "Not fizzy enough," I said.

"I heard him. Gimme that one. We'll save it for the next customer."

Cramps made another Coke, squirting in hardly any syrup and filling the cup with soda water. "Tell him they're still two bucks—including the one he sent back."

I brought the new Coke to Savard and told him what Cramps had said. Savard didn't smile or anything. He just tasted the Coke and handed it back.

"Nope. *Too* fizzy."

Cramps must have been in a good mood or something. He actually laughed when I brought the second Coke back.

"He thinks I'm joking," Cramps said. "But I'm taking it out of his pay!"

I'd forgotten all about the Chrysler and the jerk with the gorgeous girlfriend. He started flashing his lights. I went to get the tray and I saw they'd eaten the cookies.

"That'll be nine-sixty. Plus a dollar-eight for the cookies," I said.

He looked at me hard for a second, then started to smile.

"What cookies? I didn't order any cookies."

I have to admit, nobody had ever sprung that one on me before. "The cookies on the tray. You ate them, right?"

He threw his hands up and grinned even wider. "I didn't order any cookies," he said. "How could I have eaten cookies when I didn't even order any?"

He looked right at me. I looked over at his girlfriend, and she looked right at me and said, "What cookies? We didn't order any cookies."

Savard and them must have heard what was going on, because they started in sort of chanting, "Coooookeeeeee, coooooookeeeeee...." Only it was more of a grunt than a chant. Real low, like growling. I couldn't help but grin myself.

"C'mon," I said. "There were two packages of cookies on that tray. I remember putting them there."

The bald ape stopped grinning. "Why'd you put cookies on our tray if we didn't order any cookies?"

I looked over at her again, and she wasn't smiling anymore. I looked for the cellophane wrappers on the tray and didn't see any. I decided to leave the tray where it was and go back and tell Cramps what was happening. Let him decide what to do, since the cookie trick was his screwy idea. Cramps's face got white with rage when I told him the Chrysler had refused to pay for the cookies.

"You go out there and collect," he said, pointing. His eyebrows seemed even more mussed up than ever.

Fortunately, the guy in the Chrysler was smiling again and so was the girl. I couldn't believe her teeth. I mean, they were perfect.

"I'm sorry, but you've got to pay for the cookies."

The guys in my Olds started up again. "Coooooo-kee...."

I turned around and asked them if they didn't see cookies on that tray.

I couldn't believe it when every one of them shook their heads and said there weren't any cookies on the tray. They started laughing like hell. I turned back to the Chrysler. I tried to glance around on the seat, but the light cut off just about at their waists. I'd always wanted to do something like this guy was doing myself, but I couldn't have gotten away with it because Cramps knew me.

I leaned into the window of the Chrysler and whispered at them, "Look, I think this is great, but just tell me for my own satisfaction. Were there two packs of cookies on that tray?"

"Cookies? We didn't order any cookies."

"Did those guys over there in the Oldsmobile take them?"

The guy's face really brightened. He glanced at his girlfriend, then back at me. "Yeah," he whispered. "They snuck over here and grabbed them right off the tray."

I went over to the Olds. "Gimme the cookies."

They all looked surprised. I figured if anyone took them, it was probably Savard. He was closest. It would have been easy for him to go over and snatch the cookies while I was at the window talking to Cramps.

"A buck-eight, Savard," I said.

"Get off my ass, you friggin' little zit...."

That bit about the zit got me madder than anything Savard could have said. I snatched his hat off his head and went back to Cramps's window. When he threw his screen up, the moth that had been hanging around flew right in past him.

"Savard won't pay for the cookies he just stole from that Chrysler, so I took his hat to hold until he pays."

Cramps kept his teeth gritted, and his lips hardly moved when he spoke. His eyebrows were about to leap right off his head. He grabbed the hat out of my hand and flung it on the ground.

"I don't want no goddamn hat! I want them cookies paid for!"

I looked at the hat where it had landed in a little pool of oil that had dripped from some car. I went back to the Chrysler and tried to act calm.

"Look, give me a break will you? This whole thing with the cookies isn't my fault."

The guy had his nasty look back. "Why don't you tell folks the cookies aren't free?"

"Sometimes I do," I lied.

"Then why didn't you tell us?"

Suddenly I started feeling really sick. I thought about Savard and the other guys in the Olds and how they weren't making a sound, trying to listen to everything I was saying. I whispered again.

"Please tell me, just so I'll know. I won't say a word to the old man in there. Did you see those cookies?"

The ape hollered real loud. "I didn't order any cookies. Why don't you just take our tray so we can go?"

I started walking back to the window, steering clear of Savard's hat there in the oil, but I heard him behind me.

"Gimme back my hat, Grandma. Before I beat your head in."

I just kept walking. I was a little surprised that Savard didn't come over and get the hat himself. I hadn't realized he was scared of old Cramps, which was the only explanation I could think of.

I picked it up and set it on the sill of the window, but Cramps just knocked it on the ground again. I picked it up again and started back toward the Olds.

"Where the hell you going with that hat?" Cramps yelled.

"You said you didn't want it."

"Gimme back that hat!" Cramps stuck his hand out through the window and snapped his fingers.

I glanced over at the Olds. Savard was crouched low in the backseat, and the only thing I could see was the top of his head. In that single moment, I decided that Savard was more dangerous than Cramps, and I brought the hat back to Savard. Cramps slammed down his screen and I knew he was on his way out. Savard grabbed the hat. When he saw the oil, he pointed at me.

"You gonna pay for this," he said.

I could hear Cramps coming. He walked right up to the Olds and threw me out of the way. He stuck his hand in front of Savard's face. "Four bucks, you punk. And you're fired. For that matter, all of you are fired."

Cramps stood there a moment glaring at the guys in the car, then he glanced at me. "Not you," he said. "Just them."

Curran's foolish, pimply grin vanished. Bainard, alone in the front seat, turned red. Jumbo Julie started to cry. She was trying to save up for college. Savard just glared.

In back of me, I heard the door of the Chrysler open. When the guy got out, he was about five times bigger than I thought. He dangled the two packages of cookies in front of Cramps. Cramps tried to grab them, but the guy whisked them out of reach. Cramps tried his scowling routine, lowering his head and looking at the guy with his teeth gritted. "Gimme those cookies."

"You put them on my tray," the guy said. "They're mine now."

Cramps's fists were clenched and he shook all over. "That's what you think."

I guess Cramps must have seen the cops pull in behind the ape. They had the blue light flashing, so I knew Cramps had called them and it wasn't that they just happened to be driving by and noticed the trouble.

I was so outraged I couldn't keep my mouth shut. "Nice going, Cramps," I said.

I got in the Olds with Bainard and dropped my apron and

order pad out the window, and the change in the apron pockets spilled out onto the parking-lot. Cramps was busy with the Chrysler people and didn't seem to much care about us at that point. Bainard pulled out into the street and stopped. I wanted to get out of there, but the others wanted to watch. Cramps was pointing at the Chrysler guy and hollering to the cops. Then the Chrysler guy started hollering at Cramps. The cops moved in on him, but he shoved one of them away. They grabbed his arms and pinned him to the car, and before you knew it, they slapped on the handcuffs and started to haul him to the cruiser. He kicked at them and tried to twist away, and they took out their sticks and beat him on the head and shoulders. The girl jumped out of the car and ran at them, and one of the cops pushed her so hard she fell down. She jumped right up again, though. I heard myself holler, and one of the cops glanced over at us. Savard punched me in the back and told me to shut up.

"Let's get out of here," Curran said. "If my old man finds out, he'll kill me!"

Bainard popped the clutch, and the Olds shot forward. As we pulled away, I saw the guy start kicking at the cops again, and they finally beat him to the ground. The girl just stood there screaming. Jumbo Julie started crying again.

*****

I spent the next three or four days being amazed at how Cramps had called the cops to beat someone over two little packages of cookies. My old man kept asking me why I quit my job, but I wouldn't tell him. He finally called Cramps, and Cramps said he fired all of us because we didn't follow company rules. I had to laugh. Some company. And some rules. My old man stayed mad at me for a few days, until I found another job.

Bainard couldn't find a job that easily, so he offered to sell me his half of the car. The Olds is all mine now. That's one good thing. Jumbo Julie and Curran got jobs at the movie theatre. It's funny to see Curran in this little booth selling tickets. Julie sells sodas and popcorn and candy bars. Old Julie wouldn't look half bad if she took off about forty pounds. I mean, she really has a cute face.

Nobody, not even crazy Savard who'll probably turn out just like Cramps some day, tried to get their job back at The Winning Wheel. Word spread pretty fast at school, and all the kids stopped going there. I'd drive the Olds by once in a while just to see how much business Cramps was doing. I never saw more than one or two cars there, and I heard that Cramps was still pulling the cookie trick. You'd think he would have learned.

Without the high school kids' business, The Winning Wheel folded before the year was out. It was about six months after the night the guy got clubbed that Cramps finally packed it in and moved to Florida. He always said that was where he would retire.

But here's the weird thing. About two Christmases after Cramps left town, he sent me a card. Cramps. A Christmas card. I really couldn't believe it. He wrote a little note and said he heard I'd graduated fourth in my class and got a scholarship for college. He said he was really proud of me and went on to say he always thought I was the only one out of that whole crowd who was worth a shit. He actually wrote *shit* on a Christmas card. I wondered how he heard I'd graduated fourth, so I asked the others if they'd ever heard from old Cramps. They just laughed.

The Race for Last Place

On the day of each meet during the long cross country season, Daniel had felt as if he were carrying a lead vault in his stomach from the time he got up in the morning until he was actually running. He had one fear: to come in last. In his first meet he had discovered that many of the runners could be beaten in the last half mile. He had come in twenty-seventh in a field of fifty. In the second meet he had come in twenty-first.

In the third meet he discovered the technique that allowed him to quell forever his fear of coming in last. At the starting line, Daniel had let everyone go before he began to run. Watching the sixty other runners jammed all together at the starting line then surging away from him, Daniel said to himself, there, you're last. Now go! He began to catch and pass others in the long line that stretched itself around the football field and back toward the woods. With each runner Daniel passed, his pace grew quicker, his breathing fresher and deeper. In the last quarter-mile alone he passed sixteen runners and finished fifteenth. Had the race been longer, Daniel knew he would have placed even better. He could have easily run another three miles—or twenty-three. He especially loved to pass the leggy basketball players. He was one inch over five feet and weighed ninety-eight pounds, but he always beat the basketball players.

Father Paloski, the coach, looked at Daniel with mild scorn after each meet and said, "You don't punish yourself, Boucher. You might be good at this if you'd punish yourself just once. I've never seen you look tired after a race."

"I'm just in great shape, Father."

Father Paloski never allowed himself the slightest flicker of a smile, standing as always with his hands jammed into the pockets of his long, black coat, the visor of his black fedora hat pulled low over his eyes, his lips mashed so tightly together they were white.

The only runner on the team Daniel had ever heard Paloski praise consistently was Stanley Ward, who threw up after each race. And once Paloski praised Michel Minard. In that meet, skinny, bow-legged Michel Minard had led a field of forty people to within two hundred yards of the finish line before he caved at the knees and ended up having to limp to the end, finishing twentieth. Daniel, who had started the race as the last man, finished twenty-first. Michel Minard was gaunt, with a caved chest, bony legs, and thick glasses. He ran with pain burned into the squints and creases of his face and the set of his jaw. Michel had looked that way since first grade, Daniel recalled.

Serious beyond his years, Daniel's father had once remarked.

Michel and Daniel had been forced to know each other all their lives, since their fathers were both foremen at the paper mill and often watched football together on TV. Each fall, as Michel's father began to come around on Saturday afternoons, Daniel's father hinted that Daniel and Michel should become friends, that they would be good for each other. Daniel had never felt an interest in Michel; he was funny looking and quiet, very likely weird.

"You two could speak French together," Daniel's father said.

"Wow, I can't wait," Daniel wanted to reply. But he said nothing. Nor did he and Michel become friends.

*****

By the time the team bus reached Bangor, the sky was grayer and colder than it had been in Portland. Rain seemed certain, and Daniel hated running in the rain, the paths muddy and the grassy fields like swamps. They arrived at the university field house long before Daniel could fully accept being there. He was the last one to leave the bus, and only then when Father Paloski knocked on Daniel's window from outside the bus.

They were shown a section of lockers to change in, then they hung around the field house for an endless hour along with runners from sixty other schools. The competition was divided into two meets, one for the big schools and one for the small schools. The two groups gravitated toward the two ends of the field house to wait for the meet to begin.

Finally, two assistant coaches from the university cross-country team came to lead the runners around the three-mile course—

through its hills and fields and ravines and muddy power line trails. Daniel followed along in a trance, hardly noticing anything except the little red flags that marked the trail. He began to feel even more nauseated than he had on the bus, and now he felt a headache coming on, too.

He went back inside the field house and sat on the floor with his head between his knees until the dizziness went away. When the starting gun for the small school race went off, Daniel heard the collective grunt of the runners and pictured the bright swish of their nylon running shorts. Daniel blocked his ears. He felt drained and weak, and he began to wonder if he would be able to get up off the floor, let alone run, when the time came for his own race. His stomach tightened with hunger; the team had eaten breakfast but skipped lunch. He felt his tense thighs and calves and tried to massage them supple again, numb again. His legs seemed spindly, which made him think once more of Michel Minard.

Michel's family spoke French at home. Michel's grandmother had refused to learn English. Daniel's grandmother also knew little English, but that didn't motivate Daniel to learn French. To him, French wasn't a language to speak; it was the language the old folks in your family spoke. You answered in English. No one with any sense tried to answer his grandmother in French.

*****

Daniel's thoughts wandered back to the runners out on the course, and he pictured them clambering up the bank of the creek onto the power line trail, up that big hill through the apple orchard. He felt their collective strain in his thighs. "I hate this," he said aloud.

When he heard cheering outside, Daniel knew that the first runners must be coming into view, heading for the finish line. It was sooner than he'd expected, and he realized once more that his own race was only a few minutes away. Anticipating a cross-country meet made him feel the same as if he were on his way to see the dentist.

Seamans, the only senior on the team, appeared in the doorway. "Oh, there you are. Want to come watch?"

"I'll be out in a second."

Seamans didn't move, so Daniel decided that he might just as well go ahead and watch. The dampness and the cold woke him up again as they crossed the field to a corridor of people that had formed along the final stretch. Across the wide meadow, Daniel could see the first runners winding through the tall grass. Three runners had just come into view, and the crowd cheered whenever another runner appeared out of the woods and fields. Daniel realized that he'd never watched a cross-country meet; he'd only run in them.

The leaders loomed closer. It would be a tight race. Days later, Daniel would read in the newspaper that the three runners leading the small school conference had created a much publicized rivalry that year. The state meet was to be their showdown.

As they came closer, Daniel realized that one of them was screeching, taunting the others like a crow. The crowd laughed.

"Dupont," someone said. "Dupont," the others echoed.

"Paul DuPont...*il est fou celui-la.*"

Everyone laughed as the runners beat closer.

"There's no money for football at most of these small schools," Father Paloski had told them on the bus. "Cross-country's the only fall sport. All the studs run."

The two lead runners seemed no more than an armstretch from each other, and Daniel studied their legs as he waited for their faces to come into view, the lines of mouths and brows first, materializing out of the mist, then jaws and matted hair. Dupont was dark and bent, a full step ahead of Fornier, whose face was frantic, both of them hammering at the ground and the mist with their feet.

"Yeeeeeech Yeeeeech!"

The crowd laughed again. Dupont and Fornier drew within a football field's length of the finish line. To Daniel, they looked as terrified as horses in a barn fire. Fornier, with a last yelp, lowered his head and surged past the other, flashing over the line just inches in the lead. The crowd roared, startling Daniel with its size and volume. He had never seen so many people watch a cross-country meet. At least five hundred people, he thought. The third runner finished, nearly unnoticed, a single step behind DuPont and Fornier, and Daniel watched him collapse and roll on the ground as his body curled up and heaved. A steady procession formed along the finishing stretch. Small clusters of two to five runners battled for position, each of them as if he were leading the whole pack, but Daniel could not take his eyes away from the neglected third-place runner, still convulsing on the ground—ignored in spite of having lost the race by less than a second. Daniel realized that he was watching more than one race, that he was watching eighty-seven races, each with its own agony. In the big school race there would be one hundred and sixty agonies—*two* hundred and sixty, counting his own.

Far down the field, two more runners were straggling in, and he heard someone say these were the last two. These were the ones Daniel most wanted to observe. The next to last runner continued to trot, although his limbs flopped as if in slow motion. But the last racer made no pretenses; he walked. He was a stocky kid, and as he came nearer, Daniel could see that his flesh jiggled as he walked, and that his thick, black body hair was matted against his skin. One or two people clapped, but the idea of clapping angered Daniel. To clap now was to rub the guy's face in his own defeat. But the guy was smiling. Daniel was stunned. How could he come in last in front of five hundred people and smile? The sight made Daniel shiver.

*****

"Wake up, Boucher," Father Paloski said. He held several sweatsuits over his arm and snapped his fingers at Daniel. "Give us the duds."

They huddled for the prayer, kneeling on a single knee.

"In the name of the Father, and of the Son, and of the Holy Ghost, amen," Paloski intoned, his eyes clamped shut. "Heavenly Father, we know we are nothing without thy continual and eternal love. Today, we beg thee for strength such as we have never known, so that in thy wisdom and kindness, thou shalt allow thine only Jesuit representative in the state meet to register a third or fourth place, in spite of our regular season record. In the name of the Father, and of the Son, and of the Holy Ghost, amen."

The amens echoed quietly.

When they all stood up, Paloski slapped Eddie Murphy's butt. Murphy was the team captain.

"I'm depending on you, Murphy" Paloski said gravely. Then he slapped Daniel's shoulder. "Try to stay right behind Murphy."

The runners lined up, Daniel in the third tier. He felt queasier than ever as he looked down the long, chaotic line of colored running suits. The rain had quietly resumed in single drops that distracted Daniel as he tried to count them.

"On your mark..."

Daniel's stomach fluttered as he tried to concentrate on Eddie

Murphy's feet, which were directly in front of him.

"Get set..."

Daniel swayed, his vision blurred on the wall of hairy legs in front of him. The raindrops fell on his neck and arms. Eight...nine... "Go!"

*****

A pistol shot cracked. The runners thundered away from him, but Daniel stood still, bent over, full of sick stomach, ready to faint. As his knees buckled, Father Paloski grabbed his arm.

"Are you all right, kid?"

"Yes. Let me go!"

"Don't run if you're sick, Boucher."

"I'm not sick, Father. Let me go."

Paloski released his arm, and Daniel sped after the retreating runners. The moment his legs and arms were in motion, he no longer felt sick. Being last caused him no panic; it was a familiar position, after all, and he watched the other runners fade among the trees at the end of the field. In a few moments, he had crossed the field and entered the woods, where it was warm and quiet. He was ready to catch someone, but the wet leaves on the path were slippery, and he fell twice before he got to the creek bed. The sharp incline from the creek bed up to the power line trail slowed him to a crawl, and he realized with the first inkling of desperation that he was already exhausted.

At the top of the hill he regained his momentum and was once again ready to pass someone, but there was no one to pass. He ran a little harder, knowing he'd catch up to someone soon. It had worked that way all year. But his old fear of coming in last began to gnaw in a way he had not known since the first race of the year.

As he topped one hill, he caught a glimpse of another yellow uniform, like his. Steve Dennis, Daniel guessed. He'd just step up the pace until he caught Steve, then they could coast. Steve's sister, Barbara, was a year younger than Daniel. Daniel had been cultivating a friendship with Steve Dennis since the beginning of the year because he wanted to be near the head of the line to ask Barbara out next year, when her parents had said they would allow her to date.

Daniel found himself going a little too fast down the back-side of the hill, and he lost his feet and tumbled down a long stretch that was awash with mud. Back in the woods again, he

scraped his leg and arm on a broken branch. When Daniel finally caught up to Steve Dennis, it was not Steve Dennis; it was
Michel Minard. Daniel caught him midway up the hill through
the apple orchard. Michel's face was grim and exhausted.

"I thought...I was the...last one," he gasped, his face solid red.

Something else was different about his face, but Daniel wasn't
exactly sure what.

"You almost...were. I thought I was going...to black out at
the...starting line."

They ran together for a hundred yards or so, but then Daniel
was conscious of having slowed down. He wanted to catch and
pass someone else.

"Well...see ya." Daniel moved a few yards ahead but the sound
of Michel's feet didn't fade. Michel's breathing was so close behind him that Daniel began to think he could feel it on his neck.

Their momentum was disrupted by their descent into the ravine, where they had to step carefully along the wet logs and
rocks. As soon as the course uncurled into a flat path through
the woods, Daniel sprinted to get away from Michel. The soft
path was padded with pine needles that dampened their footfalls,
so Daniel was startled to discover Michel right behind him.

"You should come...over and see my...workshop sometime,"
Michel panted. "My dad and me...we set it up."

Daniel couldn't imagine where Michel got the energy to talk.
Michel edged alongside him again, and Daniel suddenly realized
what was different about him."

"Where are...your glasses?"

"I dunno," Michel gasped.

No wonder he's following me so closely, Daniel thought. He
probably can't see a damned thing. They topped a final hill, and
the athletic complex lay like a small city below them. They could
hear the crowd beginning to cheer, and Daniel realized that the
lead runners were already near the finish line.

I could trip him if he tries to pass me, Daniel thought as
Michel's feet whispered closer and closer. But Michel darted ahead
without hesitation, and Daniel saw that it was still a race to him.
Daniel surged a little harder to keep up. It was too soon to start
the final sprint, he told himself. But watching Michel once again
put yards between them, Daniel realized with anguish that the
usual rules would not apply today. In moments, he was running
harder than he'd run all year. His lungs burned and his rubbery

legs ached from his toes to his hips.

The waiting crowd saw them and began to cheer. Daniel lowered his body and closed his eyes. His feet skidded on the muddy, beaten track, but he made his knees hammer harder, his feet pound faster in the slippery mush under them. With his eyes closed, all of Daniel's mediocrities flashed before him—his lousy grades, his acne, which made girls shy away when he tried to talk to them. His ability to waste enormous quantities of time. Doing what? He did not know. Playing computer games. That was a big one. Reading comic books. Fifteen years old and still reading comic books! Putting plastic golf balls on his bedroom rug for hours at a time. He would win the Masters one day. He had yet to break one hundred on the golf course, but he could lie back and picture himself knocking in a fifty-foot putt for the win. The crowd roaring its approval....

The crowd noise grew louder, and when Daniel opened his eyes, he saw that the finish line was in sight, the waiting crowd looked bigger than a Chinese army—and Michel was still a half-step ahead.

Tackle him, Daniel thought. Trip him. Grab his shirt. Shove him. Anything!

They were only the length of a football field away from the finish line. With every step, Daniel tried to surge. He managed to pull alongside Michel, then a step ahead. The wall of bodies that formed the corridor to the finish line seemed to close toward them as Michel's long arms flailed back into Daniel's periphery. He felt Michel edging by him again.

No, Daniel screamed inside himself.

The crowd noise crashed like the ocean in his ears. Michel gained an arm's length twenty yards from the finish line. Daniel closed his eyes again, ordered his exhausted legs to pump faster, his heart to pound harder. His eyes flashed open, and he heard himself cry out as he leapt at the finish line. He hit the dirt hard, rolling and rolling. His knotted stomach and aching chest pulled him into a tight ball on the ground, and he wondered if he would ever breathe again. The blackness in his eyes grew like a dark pool. But he did not go completely black. The din in his ears sorted itself into voices. Daniel tried to roll away, but Father Polaski grasped his wrists and pulled him to his feet.

"Good show, Boucher! Outstanding, in fact. That's the first time I've ever seen you run with conviction. But let's keep moving. Don't let your muscles tighten up."

Once he was on his feet, Daniel felt something akin to relief. He stumbled toward Michel, whose face was streaked with sweat, his bloodshot eyes filled with tears. They hugged as the loud-speaker boomed their names and the positions in which they finished.

"Great race, *mon ami*," Daniel panted. "Hell of a race."

Michel nodded. Daniel wanted to cry too, but not yet. Not until the next day, when the Bangor paper would run a picture of Daniel leaping through the air at the finish line. The photo caption would say that the best duel in the entire meet was the race for next to last place. Then Daniel would remember how badly he had *wanted* to cry, for Michel but mostly for himself— but he would smile instead.

"Come on," Daniel said nudging Michel back toward the trail. "Let's see if we can find your glasses."

Father Paloski and the others followed. Paloski held them both around the biceps and raved his praise as they walked.

Nick the Russian

Nick the Russian's towels never looked used. Benjamin would go into Nick's unlocked room to snoop around, and the towels always felt clean and dry. It struck Benjamin as neither good nor bad, right nor wrong, that Russians didn't bathe. But what did surprise him the first time he let himself into Nick's room was the small crucifix on the dresser. Benjamin's fifth grade teacher had said that Russians didn't believe in God.

Nick had three books, all in Russian, and a shoebox full of letters, also in Russian. Benjamin fingered the strange cyrillic characters and admired the Russians for writing everything in an impenetrable code. An old gray suit hung alone in the empty closet, and Benjamin searched the pockets for evidence of Nick's espionage activities and found a few more letters and realized that it would be impossible, without a translator, to know how much spying Nick was actually doing.

Under the bed was the locked suitcase that had tormented Benjamin from the first day he found Nick's door unlocked. At the time, Benjamin was dry-mopping the rooms for Mrs. Donovan, the landlady. Each time Benjamin stole into Nick the Russian's room, he pulled the suitcase out just far enough to see if it were still locked. It always was.

The drawer of Nick's nightstand contained postcards of Niagara Falls, the New York skyline at dusk, Mount Rushmore and the Grand Canyon. There was a bar of soap, a toothbrush and a small tube of toothpaste. Nick did not use deodorant, as Benjamin's mother had whispered once after they passed him on the stairs. Nick's room now smelled of that same woolen, bearded odor. Nick always tipped his black Russian fur hat at Benjamin and his mother, but he did not speak. Benjamin's mother had said that Nick was a displaced person. She went on to explain about how the people in Eastern Europe didn't want to be under the Communists, and that many of them had escaped to America but couldn't become citizens until they had been here a long time.

It was ten years now since World War II was over, and Benjamin had concluded that if Nick wasn't a citizen yet, it must be because he was a spy. Benjamin thought of himself as a counter-spy and often followed the tenants of the rooming-house where he and his mother lived.

Most of the roomers led eventless lives, going from the rooming-house to work in their offices or factories each day, then spending evenings and weekends in their rooms listening to their radios. The only roomer who went to a variety of places was Nick the Russian. Benjamin always knew when Nick was leaving his room, one floor below, and he could then grab his coat and run out of the house to follow him. Benjamin's mother was used to her son's wanderings and didn't attempt to restrain him unless it was after his nine o'clock bedtime. But Nick the Russian was in his own bed by nine. It was in the afternoon that Benjamin followed him. The Russian walked so fast that Benjamin had to run to keep up with him. Nick would walk down to the docks where the Swedish and Greek and sometimes Russian ships came in, and Nick would holler up to the crew members gathered on the deck. Nick the Russian seemed to know how to holler hello in any language. He was thin and usually quiet, but Benjamin had once followed Nick to a shoestore and watched from across the street as Nick talked, throwing his hands up and leaning way back with laughter. Benjamin later found out that the people who owned the shoestore were Russians, too. It was obviously the headquarters for all the local spies, Benjamin concluded.

Most evenings when he wasn't following Nick the Russian or one of the other roomers, Benjamin cooked canned beef or chicken stew on the hot plate in their room so that there would be something for his mother to eat when she got home from work. She would eat cheerfully, telling Benjamin that he was a good cook for a ten-year-old, but Benjamin always wished there was something better for her to eat.

One night a week there was something better; on Fridays they ate at Bentley's restaurant. The streetside wall was a large window, and Benjamin often watched the people passing outside who glanced in at the diners.

"Eat your soup," his mother urged.

"It's too hot, Mom."

"It's the same as mine and mine's stone cold."

"You like soup better than I do."

"You're just waiting for the ice cream," she'd say.

"So are you."

She chuckled. "I'll never get a man if I get fat on ice cream, will I?"

"You might get a fat man,"Benjamin said, smiling.

She feigned gruffness. "Eat your soup!"

He dawdled over the soup some more, hoping the waitress would come and take it away.

"Did you have a good day at work?" he asked.

She smiled. "I had a little surprise. I was sitting in the park with a friend eating my sandwich at noon. There were lots of birds around, not just pigeons and seagulls, but a robin. First sign of spring. All of a sudden I looked up, and a man was taking a picture. Then he came over and gave me his card and said he wanted to use the picture in the paper with just a line or two about how it was almost like spring today."

"Neat."

She laughed. "I kind of enjoyed it. I haven't had my picture in the paper since I was in high school."

"Did they ask you a lot of questions?"

"Not really. Just my name and where I worked"

"So you didn't tell him about me and my detective business?"

"No, dear."

Just then Benjamin saw Nick the Russian pass by outside the restaurant. Nick didn't look in, but Benjamin recognized his hat—the only one like it in Portland. He jumped up from the table and ran toward the door.

"You sit down at this table and finish your soup."

Benjamin ran out into the cold, looking hard down the empty street where the giant snowflakes now floated in the glow of the street lights, erasing the warm, springlike day. Nick had already disappeared around a corner. Maybe he was going to the shoestore, Benjamin thought. But no, the shoestore would be closed by now. He wondered if the Russian spies had another, more secret meeting place.

Back inside the restaurant, Benjamin's mother had finished

his soup, as he had hoped she might.

"You never do a single thing I tell you," she said.

"Yes I do...." Benjamin shivered.

"I'll bet you caught a cold, running outside like that without your jacket. I don't know why you can't ever sit still. Don't you know that curiosity killed the cat?"

"I'm not a cat, I'm a detective."

"Eat your fish."

"I hate fish, Mom. Can we bring it home with us?" He shivered again.

The ice cream came after Benjamin choked down half of his fish and the waitress took away the remainder to wrap it in wax paper. When she brought it back, Benjamin's mother put it in her purse.

"There you go, shivering again...."

*****

The picture was on the front page of the paper the next morning. Benjamin's mother went to Steiner's corner store and bought three copies. Benjamin thought the picture made her look younger than she really was.

"Are they going to pay you for being in the paper?"

"No, dear."

"Too bad. It's a nice picture."

On Sunday Benjamin had not only the sniffles and a cough, he had a light fever, too. His mother made him stay in bed. She wrote letters all day, sitting at the card-table with its plastic table cloth. Benjamin wandered between sleep and non-sleep, sometimes hearing the radio and sometimes not. He dreamed about his father, out cold in a lifeboat as the ocean tried to eat him and the two other men in the raft and even the scallop boat that had brought them straight into the sudden North Atlantic storm. Benjamin no longer thought of his father's death as an empty tragedy; now that Benjamin was a detective, he thought of the episode as a mystery to be solved. So did the Coast Guard. According to their report, one of the two other men in the lifeboat said that Castor Savage had come ashore with them, and the other said Castor was washed away. So, Benjamin's mother had not, two years later, received any insurance money. It was a mystery to be solved.

When Benjamin did wake briefly from his haze, it was to sneeze or cough. Then he would start to shiver again and have to hold perfectly still to make it stop before his mother noticed and got her worried look. The next day Benjamin was still sick, and his mother decided to keep him home.

"There's cough syrup there for you, and ginger ale and orange juice in the refrigerator. Drink lots of liquids and make yourself go to the bathroom so you'll wash all of those cold germs out of you. I'll ask Mrs. Donovan to make you some lunch."

She bent to kiss him and whispered that he was her baby boy, which made him cringe. Then she was gone. He listened to her footsteps descend the stairs. Even before the outside door shut, Benjamin was out of the bed and opening the window to feed the seagulls. The sun was back, but it was a cold March sun, and Benjamin knew he should work quickly before he got another chill. He sliced a pear onto the slate roof just outside the dormer window and watched as the pigeons and gulls peck. When he closed the frosted window, the birds pecked at the glass, begging for more food. But Benjamin was no longer interested in the birds. He put on his too-big bathrobe and stupid knitted slippers and snuck downstairs to check the rooms he knew would be empty.

Dave Cook's room smelled of beer, and beside his dresser stood two grocery sacks of empty bottles. Sometimes Dave cashed the bottles in himself, but usually he gave them to Benjamin to cash in. Benjamin counted the bottles—twenty-two new ones. Eleven beers on Saturday and eleven on Sunday. Benjamin always kept track of how many beers Dave drank each night.

The Fords, who owned the coffee shop across the street where Dave worked as a dishwasher, always kept their door locked. The Fords had their own towels and linen, which they sent out to be cleaned with the restaurant's laundry. Mrs. Ford did her own dry-mopping, so Benjamin had only once glimpsed the inside of their room, a time when Mrs. Donovan asked him to deliver a telephone message. Mrs. Ford opened the door a crack. The curtains were pulled, the room was dark. Benjamin could barely see what looked like stacks of cardboard cartons arranged haphazardly along the walls, and he fiercely wondered what was in them.

He listened for a moment at Nick the Russian's door before he opened it and went in. He glanced around, noting everything in its place. A pair of plastic-looking cheap dress shoes sat atop the doily-covered maple dresser. Benjamin inspected the shoes carefully, feeling for a false bottom in the soles where the Russian might have hidden stolen government documents. Benjamin checked the nightstand drawer for new letters before he bent down to pull out the suitcase. He was so accustomed to seeing it locked that he began to push the suitcase back under the bed before he noticed that the pad lock was not fastened.

His hands trembled as he pulled the faded blue canvas valise out far enough to open the lid. Lying on top of several folded shirts was a writing pad. When Benjamin picked up the pad to check for secret messages, his mother's picture from the newspaper fluttered out from between the pages.

He stared for several moments at the clipping on Nick's small, stained rug. His heart felt like a tight harness on his chest, and his hands trembled as he replaced the clipping, set the pad back on the shirts, and closed the suitcase.

Benjamin went back upstairs and stared out the window at the pigeons and gulls that once again pecked at the glass, demanding more pear and crackers. For the rest of the morning he could think of nothing else but his mother's picture in Nick the Russian's suitcase, wondering what interest an international spy could possibly have in a woman who worked in an office. Benjamin wasn't sure exactly what work his mother performed in her office, but he decided he would have to find out.

At noon he descended the carpeted steps to eat lunch with Mrs. Donovan. He sat at the table while Mrs. Donovan, an erect old woman who wore an absent smile, cooked grilled cheese sandwiches.

"Mrs. Donovan, where'd that Russian guy come from?"

"Russia."

"No, I mean, has he lived here very long? In this house?"

"About a year, maybe."

"Do you think he might be a spy for the Communists?"

She laughed, closing her eyes for a moment. "No, honey. He's just a poor Russian immigrant. He works by the day loading trucks down at the docks. If he's a spy, he's a good one because I never would have guessed it."

He was worse than a spy, Benjamin thought all afternoon as he sat at his desk, unable to concentrate. He had decided to go to school rather than sit alone in his room or play canasta with Mrs. Donovan. As the afternoon wore on, the pit in Benjamin's stomach grew until there was nothing else inside him.

*****

During the next few days, Benjamin began following Nick

the Russian more closely, but Nick usually arrived home shortly after Benjamin got out of school, and when he did go out, it was seldom farther than the corner store for toothpaste or popcorn, or to the shoe cobbler's to see his Russian friends. Benjamin used part of his week's beer bottle money to buy a pair of toy glasses for disguise and wore his hood up as he boarded a bus marked "Munjoy Hill" that Nick got on one afternoon. Benjamin sat in the front of the bus and Nick sat in the back. But Benjamin lost him when Nick got off by the rear door at a stop near the end of the line. Benjamin was looking at a theatre marquee when he noticed Nick walking quickly along the sidewalk. The bus was already pulling back out into the traffic.

Benjamin suspected that Nick knew he was being tailed and was being especially evasive. A thought had begun to occur to Benjamin, but it seemed too outlandish even to consider. Why would the Russian have Mrs. Savage's picture in his suitcase? Because he wasn't really a Russian at all; he was Castor Savage, Benjamin's father, in disguise. Once the insurance claim was settled, they would all move to a different place—England, maybe, or Argentina—and live a life of luxury. The thought excited Benjamin and instilled in him an unbearable interest in Nick's every move.

On the other hand, Nick was just too convincing as a Russian, and the thought of Benjamin's mother's picture in a spy's suitcase was nothing short of alarming. He decided that vigilance was all he could offer in the way of investigative services. He also decided that keeping track of Nick might be impossible, and that the best thing was to begin following his mother in case he needed to protect her. But she only went to work and came back home, and Nick mostly seemed to do the same. Benjamin would follow Nick from the docks in the early afternoon, then double back to the office building where his mother worked and follow her home, catching up to her for the last two blocks.

"What have you been up to?" she always asked.

"Working on a case."

"The same case you're always working on?"

"Not sure. Might be both."

While he was cashing in his Saturday bottles the next weekend, Benjamin saw Nick leave the house and followed him to the drugstore two blocks away, where he again boarded the Munjoy Hill bus. Benjamin hurried back home and found his mother just leaving to do her Saturday errands. Then, she said, she was going to meet a friend for lunch. What friend, Benjamin almost asked, but he didn't want to appear overly curious.

"What are *you* going to do?" she asked.

"Go to the library."

"Anything you want at the store?"

"Pears."

"I mean something you don't *always* want?"

"Pie."

"All right. That sounds good. Blueberry pie, I'm sure."

Benjamin walked in the opposite direction until she rounded the first corner, then he reversed direction to follow her. He realized that she was the only one of all the roomers whom he'd never followed, except home from work. She went first to the Rexall drugstore, where she sat at the soda fountain and ate a sundae. Benjamin slipped into the store with three nuns and hid behind a postcard rack and watched her. From the drugstore, she crossed the street to the post office to mail her week's worth of letters. Benjamin smiled. His mother wouldn't use the mailboxes; she insisted that a letter wasn't mailed until you went to the post office and placed it in someone's hand. She chatted a moment with the postal clerk, who was a balding, open-mouthed man of about her age. Something she said made the clerk laugh. Benjamin watched from a phone booth.

From the post office she headed down Congress Street through the crowd of Saturday shoppers, stopping frequently to look in the store windows. When she got to Immaculate Conception Cathedral she went in. Benjamin stayed at the back of the church while his mother went up to the altar rail, put some coins in a metal box, lit a candle and kneeled on the cushion that ran the length of the railing. The footsteps and whispers of the four other people in the church crackled quietly through the large, domed silence. Benjamin was restless in no time. He wished his mother would finish praying and get on with whatever it was she did when she went out for Saturday errands. He pushed open the heavy church door, then crossed the street and crouched behind a tree to wait.

When his mother came out of the church, she wore a small, contented smile, and Benjamin guessed she had probably talked to one of the nuns. Benjamin watched her wait beside a telephone pole that was painted with the bus stop stripe. She moved nearer the edge of the sidewalk as the bus approached. Benjamin didn't know what to think when he saw that the bus she was about to board was marked "Munjoy Hill." He knew he couldn't get on the bus with her, so he ran along Congress Street behind it, staying far enough away that she wouldn't see him if she happened to look out the window. Benjamin easily kept up with the bus until the main stretch of the street where the traffic lights were synchronized. Then the bus sped far ahead, eventually disappearing into the traffic. By the time Benjamin caught it ten minutes later, the bus had turned back toward the center of town. The lone passenger was not his mother.

*****

Benjamin started back home, disappointed and angry with himself. As he walked, his eyes searched the windows of the wooden apartment buildings along his street. The spring warmth made him feel colder even than the chilly weather of the previous week.

It occurred to him that maybe this time he would catch more than a cold; maybe this time it would be pneumonia, and Benjamin knew that people sometimes died from pneumonia. And if he didn't die, he might need a long convalescence, very likely in an orphanage, since his mother turned up dead, leaving a sick and possibly dying child with only strange aunts and uncles in Massachusetts to live with. He would prefer the orphanage, he decided, provided that the police gave him any choice in the matter. Benjamin assumed that it was the police who determined where orphaned children went.

On the other hand, if Nick the Russian was really Castor Savage, his father, it would be a mistake to report whatever was going on to the police. Nick might be sent to prison for pretending he was dead, and the insurance scam would crash and burn. Then again, wasn't it illegal to try to collect insurance money on a living person? Benjamin twisted with confusion. His father was too ordinary a man to disguise himself as a Russian.

He felt much sicker than he had the week before when he stayed home from school. As he rounded the corner onto his own street, he had a vision of his rooming house in flames, with Dave Cook and the Fords and Mrs. Donovan leaping from the windows to escape. Benjamin mounted the steps, then turned the key noiselessly in the outside door. Once inside, he began to shiver uncontrollably. His teeth clattered so hard he thought they would break. He held himself tightly until the shivering stopped, then started up the stairs.

There were more sounds in the rooming house on Saturdays: Dave with his radio, George Harris with his new TV, Roger Tremblay with his radio set on a different station than Dave's. Benjamin paused long enough to concentrate on the sounds coming from each second-floor room, avoiding even a glance at Nick the Russian's door lest he be tempted go inside. For once, Benjamin thought such an act invasive.

He continued up the stairs to his own room. The room looked so neat, after his mother's Saturday morning cleaning, that it seemed almost empty. Benjamin looked at the hot plate and wished he'd learned to cook better for her. When a pigeon pecked at the window, Benjamin began to cry a little, thinking that from now on it would be just him and the pigeons and gulls. He opened the window and emptied a box of crackers on the ledge. In moments, two dozen birds were there, flapping and cooing and jostling for the crackers.

When Benjamin caught another chill, he closed the window and just watched. He thought about his mother's picture in Nick the Russian's suitcase and wondered if Nick kept pictures of his other victims. They could be good evidence, Benjamin thought. On the other hand, perhaps Nick kept that newspaper picture because she was his wife....

When Benjamin could stand the questions no longer, he descended the stairs to the second floor. Nick's door, as usual, was unlocked, and Benjamin let himself in. He was surprised to see Nick's suitcase and other belongings there on the bed. When Benjamin opened the drawers of the nightstand and the dresser, he found them empty. So that was it, Benjamin thought. Nick the Russian was not his father. A new likelihood arose in Benjamin's mind: his mother was about to be kidnapped to Russia and killed there! Benjamin pictured his mother impaled on a barbed wire fence in Russia with Nick the Russian beating the bottom of her feet with a hose, the way he'd read that Communists were prone to do.

The sick feeling in Benjamin's stomach swept through his arms and legs as he eyed the suitcase and paper shopping bag on the bed. He poked through the shopping bag and found only two pairs of shoes and six books, all of them in Russian. Benjamin fingered the padlock on the suitcase, but it was once again fastened.

He heard new sounds from below as the outer door closed and someone started up the stairs. Benjamin began to shake, thinking it might be Nick coming back to his room, but there were too many feet for just one person. The footsteps continued to the floor above, and Benjamin heard his mother's voice and a grunted reply that he recognized as coming from Nick the Russian. Mother was still alive, thank God, Benjamin thought. Nick the Russian hadn't killed her yet, but maybe Nick was planning to kill her there in the room. Benjamin crept up the stairs as soon as he heard the door click shut and listened from near the top of the stairwell. He heard no voices, only the sound of breathing, and Benjamin wondered what they were doing. The thought that Nick the Russian might be kissing her came to Benjamin for the first time and confused him further. His mother would not kiss another man, would she? So here was the final proof: Nick the Russian was her husband, Benjamin's father.

Now he heard muffled voices at the door, and Benjamin knew he'd better get out of sight again. The door opened just as Benjamin reached the second floor. He would have hidden in the bathroom, but it was occupied. The footsteps started down the stairs, and Benjamin slipped into the only hiding place available, Nick the Russian's room.

As soon as Benjamin had closed the door, he knew he'd made a mistake. He thought about hiding under the bed but instead slipped into the closet. When he opened the door and found Nick's old, musty-smelling suit still hanging there, he knew he'd made another bad choice, but he pulled the closet door shut behind him and crouched in the corner, hoping that maybe Nick had left the suit there because he no longer wanted it.

The door of the room opened and closed. Benjamin braced himself to be found and, if Nick was not his father, murdered. In the silence, Benjamin wondered what Nick the Russian was doing. The seconds ticked like centuries, and Benjamin was no longer sure Nick was even in the room.

Then the footsteps came quietly across the floor, and the closet door opened, letting in the sudden light. Their eyes met in sustained contact for the first time that Benjamin could recall, and his heart belted against his ribs hard enough to break them. The Russian's mouth opened but he did not speak. His unsurprised eyes bore into Benjamin for a long moment, then Nick began to smile, and the skin at the corners of his eyes creased as the smile grew. He laughed as he took his suit from the closet and stuffed it, wire hanger and all, into his shopping bag, As he started out the door, Nick laughed again and set the suitcase down while he fished a candy bar out of his pocket and held it toward Benjamin, who remained crouched in the closet.

"Like?"

Benjamin nodded. Nick tossed the candy bar onto the bed, waved, and walked out, leaving the door open behind him. Benjamin listened to his quick, light footsteps in the hallway. The downstairs door opened and closed, and Benjamin scrambled to the window to look out. Nick the Russian stepped briskly along the sidewalk, unslowed by the weight of everything he owned.

Benjamin sped up the stairs and into his room. His mother was startled and let out a small gasp. Benjamin was so relieved to see her still alive that he ran to her and hugged her. She laughed as she held him and asked him if he was still her baby boy. He didn't mind saying yes.

Later that afternoon, Benjamin ate the candy bar and wondered where Nick's headquarters was sending him for his new assignment. He didn't mention to his mother that he'd seen Nick leaving, and she never explained why she and Nick had been in the room together or anything else she might have known about Nick the Russian. The only time he ever heard her mention Nick was several years later, after Mrs. Donovan had died and Benjamin's mother had finally received her insurance money and bought the rooming house. She was explaining to a new tenant, who was Armenian, that they'd once had a Russian living there.

"He worked near my office," Benjamin's mother said. "We used to eat lunch in the park together, and once we had our picture taken for the newspaper. They cropped him out of it though and just ran my picture. I think it hurt his feelings. He dressed funny and didn't know more than twenty words of English."

For a few moments, Benjamin remembered the empty feeling he'd had when he first discovered the newspaper photo in Nick the Russian's suitcase.

"He had a crush on me, I'm pretty sure," she went on. "But it would have been just about impossible to have had much of a realtionship with him." She glanced at Benjamin, but not angrily. "He being a Russian and all....We were under almost constant surveillance."

Selling Delphinium

For three short summers of my childhood, I sold delphinium by the roadside. I know the last summer, the one just before we moved to Portland, I was eleven, but the summer I met the Leibowitz people, I was nine. From about eight in the morning until late afternoon, I'd sit at my cloth-covered card table in those breezeless June and July mornings as the cars swished by, always on their way to one of the eight lakes around our town. I was too young to realize that most of the people in the cars were on their way to work. When I was nine, everyone except me was on his way to the lake. More tantalizing yet were the pontoon planes that took off from Naples full of summer sight-seers and droned overhead in the lazy afternoons, filling me with a mild resentment of my earthbound chore.

I'm nearly positive that the delphinium stand was my mother's idea, although the one time I asked her, she insisted that the stand was my own doing. Each morning I waded among the bees and stinging grasses with my bucket of water—and the pair of large shears that terrified me, lest I fall on them—toward the wall of towering stalks that were solid with blue, trumpet-like flowers. I'd cut fifty or sixty of the flowers that wavered over my head, then plunge them into the bucket. At least three or four of the cats would follow me, attacking my dew-soaked sneakers from behind tufts of grass as I passed.

The rest of the morning, I'd sit at the card-table with my bucket, my sign and my stack of newspapers for wrapping the bunches of flowers I sold. My father, who managed a lumber mill, had taught me how to play solitaire, so the deck of cards was my main entertainment. Every hour or so, my mother would bring me an icy glass of Kool-aid and ask how business was—as if she couldn't see from the window whether or not anyone pulled

145

into the driveway. I don't remember ever selling any flowers to local people; the delphinium seemed always to be driven away in out-of-state cars by well-tanned women in sunglasses, unwrinkled white shorts, and stiff, crownless visor caps. On days when the flowers didn't sell, my mother set them in vases in our bay window, facing the road.

The first day the Leibowitzes stopped, I had sold hardly any flowers. They slowed way down in their dark green Cadillac as the woman who drove levelled the black gaze of her sunglasses on my stand. I watched the Cadillac turn around in the driveway at the foot of the hill and head back. It appeared that they were going to drive by again but at the last second, the Cadillac wrenched deftly into our yard. I waited for someone to get out, but several moments went by before anyone moved. A balding, monkeylike little old man with the largest ears I'd ever seen sat on the passenger side, his head barely at window level. I glanced at the license plate. The car was from New York. The driver finally got out and smiled at me over the roof of the car. She was not very tall, and I could see that she had to stand on her tiptoes to see me. Her face was round and full and motherly—in fact, at this short distance, she reminded me a little of my mother, with her silver-streaked hair and modest light blue, short-sleeved dress. The similarities ended abruptly when she spoke. The tone of her voice, not to mention her strange way of pronouncing words, made her seem as if she were lost and had stopped for directions.

"Hello there. What *gorgeous* flowers you have. I *love* larkspur."

I had never heard delphinium called by any other name, but I felt no urge to try to correct her. All I could manage was a grunt.

"We have larkspur in our own special garden in Yonkers," she went on. "It's the only thing we miss about New York when we come up here in the summer. But now we can have our Maine and our larkspur, too. I'm just so glad we found you."

The lady closely examined the delphinium in the bucket, and I shot a glance at the old man in the car, who stared straight ahead at my father's pickup.

"That's Pa-pah," the lady said. "He's a little hard of hearing, but he'd probably be *thrilled* if you stepped over there and said hello."

Nothing could have been more removed from my palette of

natural inclinations than to approach the Cadillac and the frowning little man inside. But then she began nudging me toward the car, whether I liked it or not. The lady rapped near the open window, and the old man jumped, turning his startled face toward us for just an instant.

"This delightful little fellow wants to say hello to you, Pa-pah."

The old man looked contemptuously at me, nodded curtly and turned away.

"Pa-pah loves to fish. He spends most of the day out in his little boat. Do you fish, too? I'll bet you do, with all these wonderful little lakes and brooks and streams."

I had been fishing only once in my life and, although I tried my best, I could not find it interesting. I came very close to actually speaking and telling the woman that, no, I didn't fish; but then she was talking to the old man again.

"Why don't you invite him to come to the lake and go fishing with you one day, Pa-pah? I'll bet he'd love that." She turned to me and smiled. "Pa-pah says he'd love to have you come." Then back to the old man, whose window began to slide shut with a dull electric hum. "Let me get some flowers first, Pa-pah. Then we can talk about it."

She bought the entire bucketful and helped me wrap newspaper around the dripping stems as she talked non-stop. Then we carried the bundles to the car and, with her key, she opened the vast, immaculate trunk. I'd never seen a clean car trunk before, and the lack of jacks, tire chains and grease-stained burlap sacks struck me as some sort of bad manners. I watched in disgruntled awe as she laid the flowers neatly on the carpeted floor of the trunk. The lid shut soundlessly.

"Now. Let me give you this for the larkspur...and this is a tip for your for being such a smart, charming little gentleman."

She handed me a ten-dollar bill for the flowers and, in the other hand, a single dollar bill. I wouldn't have charged more than five dollars for the flowers, but I felt it would be impolite to argue over the price. My mother would have argued, but I just stuffed the money in my pocket.

"Thank you"

"You're entirely welcome. Now, I'd like to speak with your mother. Is she in?"

I nodded toward the house. I wasn't sure why she wanted to

talk with my mother, but after Mrs. Leibowitz had left, I learned
that I would be going to their lakehouse the next day for lunch.

"They're very nice people Gilbert," my mother said as she
stood at the sink washing strawberries. "They're Jewish. You'll
have a wonderful time."

I'd never heard the word *Jewish* before, but its sound filled
me with an inexplicable curiosity. Jewish? Was that anything like
bluish? Or dewish?

The next morning, Mother had me ready to go at seven
o'clock. I usually didn't even get up until then, but Mrs.
Leibowitz had told Mother that she would pick me up at seven-
thirty. I spent an hour and a half sitting on the front porch glider
with my paper bag containing my swimsuit and towel when Mrs.
Leibowitz pulled in just before nine. She didn't seem to notice
me and ran into the house where she jawed with my mother for
another fifteen minutes.

The two women finally came out on the porch. The momentary resemblance that I first thought Mrs. Lebowitz and my
mother shared was in no way apparent now. My mother was un-
mistakably a pale, blotchy-skinned housewife, whereas Mrs.
Leibowitz looked aristocratically tan and almost shiny from being waited on in the sun.

Mother smiled proudly at me. "Mrs. Leibowitz says you're
one of the nicest boys she's ever met."

I felt myself turn red and saw in my mother's eyes that im-
ploring look that hoped I would say *please* and *thank you* without having to be overly prodded. I couldn't open my mouth, let
alone speak.

"He was *soooo* helpful, carrying the larkspur to the car for
me."

A silence that was void of even passing cars and distant mo-
torboat engines settled over the porch as the two women waited
for me to say something in response.

"Sometimes he's a little shy," my mother apologized.

"Ooooh, but that's what's so charming. And Pa-pah just *loves*
him."

*****

My mother kissed me goodbye and told me to make her proud
by remembering my manners. Mrs Leibowitz opened the car door
for me and I slid in. I noticed immediately that Cadillacs smell
different from other cars—as if they'd just come from some sort

of car beauty parlor. Most of the way to the lake, Mrs. Leibowitz
was silent. I had grown so accustomed to her usual barrage that I
found her silence unnerving. A short distance up the road from
my house, we pulled in at a winding, paved driveway that ended
at a small log cabin and makeshift pier, which seemed to hang
dangerously out into the lake on its spindly pilings. I was over-
come with a fierce sense of letdown in that I expected that these
rich New Yorkers would live in one of those castle-like old stone
mansions with their green-shingled roofs that so many outof-
state people had built along the lake. So the log cabin seemed
tawdry. We got out of the car, and I followed Mrs. Leibowitz
toward the shabby dock, which I quickly saw was not just shabby,
it was scary. The floorboards sagged with each step we took and
sent up the stink of creosote.

Sitting in a little rowboat tied to the end of the pier was the
old man. He was surrounded with tackle boxes, fishing rods, burlap sacks—everything that should have been in the unblemished
trunk of the Cadillac. In the center of the boat's floor was a pile
of coiled rope as big as a barrel. The old man wore a baseball cap
that had a small green plastic window cut in the long visor.

"Here he is, Pa-pah. Here's your little friend."

The way she said it made me feel as if I were being delivered
into the hands of a maniac whose plan was to bind and gag me in
the middle of the lake, then dangle me overboard for bait. I found
strange comfort in the hat, though. I figured that no one of a
respectably homicidal bent would be caught dead wearing such a
ridiculous hat.

Mr. Leibowitz held me by one hand by as I climbed down
the three-rung ladder into the boat, the first I'd ever been in. It
rocked only a little, but that was enough to make me dizzy. As
soon as I was seated in the stern, Mrs. Leibowitz stood up and
waved.

"Have fun!" She got into the Cadillac and drove away.

The boat drifted in place for several minutes as the old man
sat inertly with his back toward me, an oar across his lap. Finally, he dipped the oar into the water, and the boat began to
drift away from the pier, self-propelled, it seemed. The coiled
rope played out like a lethargic, sun-drugged snake, too slow even
to notice. When we were about fifty feet from the pier, Pa-pah
decided that it was time to fish. He handed me a fishing rod,
baited my hook, then his own, and cast his line, assuming, I guess,

that I would do the same. He watched that nearly invisible junction of line and water with an unflagging interest, and I become so engrossed in watching him that I forgot to cast my own line.

"Fish," he ordered gruffly. "Don't be watching me."

I did my best not to watch him for the rest of the morning. I dangled my line timidly into the water, trying not even to ripple the calm water in the slightest way. I remembered Mrs. Leibowitz's voice urging us to have fun. The closest thing to fun I felt was when one of the pontoon planes from Naples buzzed overhead, close enough to cast a large shadow. I longed to reach up, grab the pontoon strut, and be swept up and across the lake, like a fish snatched off by a kindly hawk.

Eventually I noticed a massive stone-pillared house rising up behind the trees near the log cabin, but I didn't connect the place with the Leibowitz people until hours later, at lunchtime. As the morning dragged on, I studied all of the houses along the shore just so that I wouldn't be watching Pa-pah. The only times I openly watched him were when he was reeling in his line to see what he'd caught. I was amazed by the deliberate, almost affectionate way he removed each fish from his line and threw it back in the lake. After the third or fourth time, he seemed to sense my dismay and muttered, "Too small."

When I finally felt a tug on my own line, the old man became excited and jabbered in a foreign language as he tried to tell me how to reel my line in. He finally grabbed the pole out of my hands and reeled the line in himself. As the fish cleared the water, he gave it a scathing look, snatched it off the hook, and threw it back. I was puzzled because I thought the fish looked much larger than the ones he had caught.

"Sunfish," he mumbled. "No damned good for anything."

We drifted in the boat, facing in opposite directions. I started thinking about how I was finally at the lake, like everyone who drives by my house towing their boats. Why did I want to be home sitting at my delphinium stand? I realized that there were no other boats out on the lake, no swimmers diving from the docks that punctuated the shoreline, and I began to think that perhaps no one really went to the lake after all. The parade of boats on their trailers and summer people who passed our house everyday were just an act meant to tantalize and confuse the locals. I told myself to ask my mother and father about it.

The old man finally caught one he considered worth keeping. To me, the fish didn't look an inch longer than the ones he'd thrown back, but Pa-pah smiled and held that fish up in front of him, first high, then low, then up close as the fish flapped itself to death. He talked to the fish in that strange language of his even after he'd dropped it in a bucket.

Then he looked at me. "Lunchtime," he said. He fished the long rope out of the water and began pulling us back to the pier, re-coiling the rope in the bottom of the boat as he tugged. In about five minutes we docked at the wobbly pier and climbed out of the boat. The old man told me to wait. He stepped inside the cabin and shut the door behind him. While he was out of sight, I found myself looking toward the long, winding driveway and plotting my escape. I knew exactly where I'd be in relation to my house once I reached the state road—turn to the left to go to town; turn right to go to my house. But I just stood there on the spot the old man had pointed to when he said, "Wait right there."

When he came out of the cabin, he picked up his bucket with the lone fish and began nudging me toward the woods. I had no idea what was going on, but we soon came to a clearing, and the stone house I'd seen from the lake loomed above me into the clouds. The old man strode up the broad steps toward the vast glass doors that faced the lake. He opened the door, then impatiently gestured for me to enter. In spite of all the furniture, the raw space of the room with its cathedral ceiling and exposed waist-thick beams seemed palatial. The first wall I noticed was almost completely covered with mounted deer and moose heads. Not realizing that the trophies were probably store-bought, I conjured an image of Mrs. Leibowitz and Pa-pah in jungle helmets and khaki field clothes, carrying submachine guns toward a covey of moose that lounged about a waterhole.

"There they are," Mrs. Leibowitz sang out. "Welcome back, fishermen! Did you catch anything? Oh, Pa-pah did. Of course. Here, give me that and I'll have Jenna cook it for you. What about our young guest? Didn't catch one? Oh well. Maybe this afternoon you'll catch one of those nice big perch like Pa-pah sometimes catches."

The prospect of spending the afternoon in the dinghy with the old man plunged my heart between my knees. I had assumed they would take me home after lunch.

"Sit right down here, Gilbert," Mrs. Leibowitz directed, pulling out a mahogony ladderback chair and patting its fancy curved top.

I sat down and tried not to stare at the strange bowls of food that covered the table. The smell of the food was totally unfamiliar, and I feared it. The only food I recognized was a bowl of carrots, but even the carrots seemed strange—a small mound of shavings instead of the neat rounds my mother always cut.

Then I saw what looked like a doughnut, and my hopes began to climb. Mrs. Leibowitz must have seen me looking at it because she took one from the basket, sliced it in half, put some white goo on it, then some slices of orange stuff, and handed it to me.

"Locks and bay gulls," she said. There were some round, browned balls that she called *fell-awfuls* (or maybe felt-awfuls; I wasn't sure). The green stuff that looked like kind of like vomit but smelled like lemons and tomatoes was *ter-bully*.

The Leibowitz people began to eat. I picked up the bay gull and sank my teeth into it but immediately realized it was not at all like a doughnut. My teeth backed out of the tough bread like a cat backing out of a paper sack. The meal went downhill from there. This, I realized, was what the word *Jewish* meant—weird food.

"Gilbert, you're not eating. Is there something wrong?"

I shook my head no and again bit into the bay gull. I chewed and chewed but could not bring myself to swallow the tough wad in my mouth, and when no one was looking, I pretended to wipe my lips and soundlessly spat the dough into the napkin.

"See what we did with your lovely larkspur?" Mrs. Leibowitz chimed, nodding toward two enormous brass urns that flanked the stone fireplace. Seeing the flowers in anything but my bucket made me feel disconnected from them, as if the flowers had been brought from New York along with the strange food and the incomprehensible language that the old man muttered to the fish he had caught.

A woman in a white uniform came into the room carrying a plate with Pa-pah's little fish on it. The old man nodded curtly and said, "Give some to the boy."

In those days, there was nothing I hated more than fish. I poked at the tiny white morsel with my fork and saw three evil little bones. Pa-pah was consuming his portion, bones and all, smiling at each bite before he forked it into his mouth. His long, birdlike visor bobbed as he chewed.

"Pa-pah does love his lunch," Mrs. Leibowitz said

Somewhere upstairs a grandfather clock pounded out the midday hour.

"Did that startle you?" Mrs. Leibowitz asked, standing up from the table. She was gone only a few minutes, and when she returned from the kitchen, she carried a new plate. She pushed the fish out of the way and set a peanut butter sandwich in its place. I wolfed it down with milk, grateful for the return of my appetite.

*****

I had hoped that Pa-pah would want a post-lunch nap, but such was not the case. We trudged back through the woods to the pier and stopped again at the cabin I'd originally thought was the Leibowitz summer home. This time the old man left the door open, and I came close enough to peer inside. The cabin was windowless and dark, and when my eyes adjusted, I saw nets and tackle boxes, stacks of old newspapers, buckets of nails, dismantled boat motors. I smelled tar and dust.

Pa-pah stood in front of a rusty mirror adjusting his hat on his head. The longer he adjusted the hat, the more serious and varied his expressions grew. I hated to see him get serious again because I was starting to like him, remembering the way he smiled when he ate his fish. By the time we were back in the boat, Pa-pah was once again completely removed from me. He untied the long rope from the pier and tossed it in the boat. Before I was even seated, he placed the oars in the oarlocks and rowed—and with a vengeance, breathing more and more noisily. I began to wonder if he was mad at me because I had not eaten the fish he offered at lunch. When we reached a spot he deemed worthy of fishing, he sat with his back to me, stooped protectively over his rod as if I might try to steal anything he caught. Pa-pah didn't bait my hook or even offer me the can of worms to bait my own hook; he simply ignored me.

It wasn't long after I'd cast my line that the barely discernible rocking of the boat lulled me to sleep. There was no way of knowing how long I slept, since the sun seemed to hang immobile in its apex all day long. I reeled my line in to check the hook, which was nibbled clean. When I reached for the worm can, I noticed that Pa-pah was slumped over the stern of the boat, his visor nearly in the water. My heart hammered in my throat, and I felt a numbing chill race through me, making every cell of me tremble. I watched for the rise and fall of his back to tell me he was still alive and breathing, but I saw only a deathly stillness.

My eyes roamed over the lake, searching for a single soul who could help me. And even though I saw no one, I screamed for help anyway, hoping more than anything that my screams would wake Pa-pah from his deep, dark sleep. It was no use. I was convinced that Pa-pah was dead, and that death, like measles, would soon spread to me if I didn't do something.

I knew I couldn't row properly, with the old man slumped where he was, so I wrestled one of the oars out of the oarlock and began to paddle, first on one side, then on the other, as I'd seen an Indian do in some movie. The boat only twisted from side to side rather than advancing toward the shore. Whenever I stopped for a few moments to rest, I studied the old man to see if he was breathing. My eyes had clouded with tears, and I could hardly see anything.

Perhaps it was the difficulty I had seeing that made me stop watching the shore. When my paddle touched ground, I looked up and saw that we were almost back to the dock. I eased myself into the water and began pulling the boat by the bow. I rammed the boat between two pilings of the shaky wharf to hold it in place, then went running for Mrs. Leibowitz. To my unspeakably enormous relief, I found her sitting on the verandah reading a magazine. I stood on the bottom step, grunting and whimpering and gesturing. The only word I could manage was *dead*! Mrs. Leibowitz came running behind me in her sneakers. "Are you sure? Are you sure?" she kept asking.

When we got to the boat, the old man had changed position, and Mrs. Leibowitz stood on the dock calling to him.

"Pa-pah! Pa-pah!"

I couldn't bear to watch it. I'd heard words from my parents like heart attack and cancer, and I was convinced that I'd spent the afternoon drifting with a dead man, who would haunt my dreams for the rest of my life.

"Pa-pah!"

"What?"

"Are you asleep?"

"Hell no...."

"You scared us, Pa-pah. Why didn't you tie your long rope?"

"Forgot."

I clearly recalled his deliberately untying the rope before we got in the boat, but I said nothing.

"He *always* ties that rope to the dock," Mrs. Leibowitz explained. "That way we can just pull him in when he falls asleep. Otherwise he drifts out into the middle of the lake, and all the hollering in the world won't wake him." She bent closer to me and whispered, "I think maybe it embarrasses him to use the rope when he has company."

*****

Naturally there was a big to-do when Mrs. Leibowitz drove me home. She went on and on to my mother about how brave and smart I was. What really got me was when she told my mother about what a good fisherman I was. My mother beamed in the shower of all the vicarious praise. There was nothing I could say, certainly not in front of the effusive Mrs. Leibowitz, to try to correct my mother's vision of the day, so I didn't even try.

I more or less forgot about the Leibowitz people until a few weeks later, when the Red Cross called my mother to say that I had been awarded some kind of certificate.

"A life-saving award," my mother said. "Something about Mrs. Leibowitz's father."

"But he wasn't dying," I said. "He was just asleep. Big time."

"I know. But Mrs. Leibowitz felt that you saved his life anyway."

So my mother and father drove me to Portland to get my certificate. I didn't want to go. I thought the whole thing was ridiculous, but my parents told me that I should always be proud of any recognition I ever got, and that I should never think that I didn't deserve it. When I told my father that the main thing I was thinking about at the time was my fear that I was riding in a boat with a dead man and just wanted to get out, he smiled and told me never to admit that to anybody. I was a late baby; my folks were already in their fifties the summer of the Leibowitz event, and I always thought his white hair and thick glasses gave him an air of unmistakable gentleness and sagacity.

"If you don't want the certificate," he told me, "then you should give it to me so I can hang it in my office at the sawmill."

I told him I'd keep it myself—that way I could make sure no one else ever saw it.

I guess we expected some kind of ceremony, with a lot of people and reporters and photographers at the Red Cross office, but, fortunately, it was nothing like that. A secretary handed us an envelope and winked at me, as if she knew what was really going on, and we left. My father and mother looked disappointed, but I was relieved.

When we got back to the car, I opened the envelope and looked at the certificate. It was about the size of a postcard—the envelope was much bigger—and really wasn't much to look at. Back home, I stuffed the envelope under some socks in my dresser. I didn't really forget about it, but I didn't take it out to look at it either. Not until the end of the summer, when we heard that Pa-pah Leibowitz had died. Sure enough, he was in his boat when it happened. According to the newspaper, he was found dangling into the water, his head submerged. I thought about how Mrs. Leibowitz used to put him out each morning with the rope tied to the boat, sort of the way you'd tie up a dog in your yard. Then I felt bad for thinking about her that way because she never struck me as mean, just too busy talking to notice things—like the fact that company was the last thing her father wanted.

It also crossed my mind that she'd never come back to buy more delphinium, and I wondered why. It turned out that Pa-pah had been sick all summer, and that the Leibowitzs had spent most of their time at a hospital in Boston.

My mother bought a sympathy card at the drugstore and had me sign my name. She got the New York address from the postmaster there in Harrison. It was the card, more than the newspaper story, that made me realize that the old man was really dead. The whole thing bothered me for about a day, then I decided that I should have my certificate framed so I could hang it on my wall. My mother seemed very pleased that I'd changed my mind about the certificate and now understood its value. She told me, if I remember correctly, that I was starting to grow up, but not too fast.

Screwdriver

Henry

Randolph is standing in the yard looking up at the sky. He does that more than anybody. And he doesn't just look in one place, 'cause his head moves around and he's looking in different places like there really is something to see. Only he does it fast, like the thing he's watching is zipping around, like a fly. Or else he isn't looking at anything at all; he just moves his head funny, like he's trying to get something out of his ears.

"Henry!"

Mother is calling me, but I'm hiding up here in the barn chamber with the hen so nobody will see what happened.

"Randolph, where's Henry?"

Randolph never answers when Mother calls him.

"Randolph, I'm talking to you."

"What, what? Jesus!"

"I asked you where Henry was."

"How the hell should I know...?"

Mother sits on the well. The tin topping creaks. "There was a time when older brothers used to look after their younger siblings."

"Ain't that just wonderful...." Randolph paces back and forth, four steps one way, then four another.

"All right. I guess it's fairly obvious that you just don't care to have me here talking to you." Mother keeps sitting there. Randolph is looking the other way into the woods.

"After all, I'm only your mother. I guess that doesn't mean anything anymore, though. When I think of how my brothers and I used to act toward my mother. Why, she was just like a queen, the way we treated her. And if we *didn't* treat her like a queen, we had my father to answer to...."

"Well now...ain't that precious."

Randolph starts to walk away. He always does when Mother is talking to him. He told her once that her voice upset his stomach. Whenever he says things like that to Father, Father bats him, but it doesn't make any difference to Randolph, and he says bad stuff anyway, and Father bats him. Randolph bats back at Father, but Father bats harder than Randolph 'cause he's older. Last year Father and Randolph got in a fight out in the yard, and Randolph gave Father a bloody nose, and Father knocked Randolph's tooth out.

"Randolph! Come back here!"

"For *Christ's* sake will you stop hollering?"

"You don't have any respect for me at all, do you?"

"What's that got to do with anything?"

Mother goes back inside and slams the door. Randolph goes toward the woods. I can look down and see everything in the yard, just like an airplane. If I had an airplane, I'd keep it up here in the barn chamber.

Now I can get out the back way with the chicken. I have to be careful or else it will bleed all over me and they'll know. I threw the screwdriver out the window into the field 'cause it was all bloody and they'd know, if they saw it.

"Henry!"

Mother is calling again, but I don't answer. I can hide the chicken in the woods. It's still a little bit alive and keeps flapping against my leg. When I whack it on the head, it stops flapping. But then I get blood on my hand. It's getting dark in the woods, so I've got to hurry and hide it.

"What in hell you got there?"

It's Randolph. He scared me.

"What is it? A hen? Look at that...what'd you do to it?"

"Nothing."

He grabs my arm and holds it up.

His eyes open real wide and he whistles. "You killed it. I'll be damned...."

I can't tell if he's mad. "Are you going to tell?"

"Why shouldn't I?"

"I'll get batted."

"Tell me why you did it and I'll decide."

"It bit me."

"Chickens don't bite. They ain't got teeth, you ninny!"

"It bit me. Honest. When I was gathering eggs."

"Hah. So you killed it."

"Yes."

"Vicious little bastard, ain't you...?"

"Are you going to tell?"

"Maybe. What'd you do, stick a knife in it?"

"A screwdriver. Please don't tell...."

"A screwdriver?" Randolph whistles again. He's funny when he laughs, and he always makes me laugh, too.

"Henryyyyyy and Raaaaandolph!"

"What'd you do with the screwdriver?"

"Threw it out in the field."

"Threw it out in the field? The old man's gonna miss it, you know. What are you going to say to him when he asks you where it is?"

"Are you going to tell?"

"Tell what? That you finished off one of his precious goddamn hens? Shame to waste a good screwdriver, though." Randolph lights a cigarette.

"You smoke!"

"No shit, Sherlock."

Now if Randolph tells on me, I can tell on him, too. It's getting darker in the woods. I can just barely see Randolph and the cigarette looks like a firefly.

"Look, what are you planning to do with that hen?"

"Does Father know you smoke?"

"Yeah. He knows. We both pretend he don't. That's the deal we worked out. One day he caught me for about the eighty-fifth time, and I was all ready to square off with him again, only he says, 'Look, I'm sick of beating your ass for smoking. Just don't do it around me and the old lady, and we'll forget about it.'"

My hands feel real sticky, and I can feel a big wet spot on my pants where I wasn't careful with the chicken.

Out there in the field, it's real dark now, and Mother is still calling.

"Are you going away to school, Randolph?"

"Hell no. I can't stand school."

"Mother told Mrs. Evans you were going away to school." Randolph makes a funny face. "That figures."

"You going in the army?"

"Not a chance."

"Then where you going? Last night I heard Mother and Father talking, and they said you were going somewheres."

"Look, what are you going to do with that foolish hen? You can't stand here holding it all night, you know."

Randolph's bedroom is right next to mine, and sometimes at night I can hear him talking to himself. But when I try to listen, I can't understand the words.

"Randolph, did you get throwed out of school?"

"Yeah."

"Did Father bat you?"

"Shit yeah."

I like talking to Randolph. He smokes and swears and makes the cigarette go in circles in the dark.

"Why don't you like Father?"

"Warren? I like him fine. I used to feel sorry for him in a way, but then I seen that what he's got himself into is his own damn fault, and if he don't want to do anything about it, that's his business. Feeling sorry for him's just a waste of time."

Randolph is quiet for a while. I count how many times—three—he puffs his cigarette. "...Like marrying that whine machine up there in the house. Every time I say something to him about it, though, he figures it calls for a fight."

Randolph doesn't say anything for a long time. I can't see him very well in the dark, but I know he's blowing smoke rings.

"You know that scar on my chin? That's what I got for trying to help him fix his carburetor. He don't know his ass from a fan belt. So I try to give him a little friendly help, and *wham*, I'm on the ground looking up. Just cause I told him he could fuck up a wet dream if he was having it under the hood of a car. And I said it real friendly, laughing and joking and all...."

"Fact is, Warren might have amounted to something better than a clerk in a five-and-dime store if he'd a been more careful picking a wife. Hell, *I* could have turned out a whole lot better. And *you*..."

Randolph starts laughing again. Then I hear the bushes crackling and see a flashlight poking along the side of the house.

"Is that you Henry? Randolph...?"

Randolph grabs the chicken out of my hand and whispers, "Here, give me that goddamn thing. Now get out of here."

Warren

"You about ready, Warren?"

"Anytime you are."

Don hit the light switch. It was pitch black 'cause the blind in the front window of the store was drawn. We had to go slow down the aisle and sort of feel our way along. I set my hand on a counter of can openers, then on a counter of salad utensils, plastic forks and stuff, and then on a counter of little boxes which could have been anything. I didn't know 'cause it wasn't my department.

"Pretty dark, eh Warren?"

Don, he's the manager. He didn't seem to be having no trouble getting around. Knows the place like the inside of his wallet. By the time I was halfway down the aisle, he was opening the door. That let in a little light. I took one last look around. The dolls all stood right up there on the counter, like they couldn't wait for us to leave.

Outside it was getting chilly. We walked around back of the store to where my car was parked. Don had to wait until I unlocked his door, then he got in a hurry, shivering.

"We'll get a little heat on in a second," I told him.

There wasn't one car on the main drag, and it was only eight o'clock. Naturally, that made me think about the way Randy was always bitching about how dead Norway was.

"How's Randy doing with his harem, Warren?"

I figured that'd come up sooner or later, knowing Don. That's all he ever thinks about—who's screwin' who. Half the time he's just as happy with who *might* be screwin' who.

"He's doing all right, I guess."

"I seen their car parked in the field down in back of my place 'bout six this morning. Sittin' at the table drinking my coffee, and I happened to look down there and seen Randy get out of the car and take a leak and then get back in."

I still hadn't seen 'em. I'd seen their car once in town with Randolph in it, but by the time I got done noticing Randolph, they were by already, going pretty fast for in town, and I didn't get much of a look at the two girls. The one that drove was blonde, that was all I saw. And I noticed the Tennessee plates. Next day Randolph says to me, "Warren, what'd you say if I was to up and go South for the winter?"

"He's doing all right, I guess." I nodded at Don. "I hear enough about him through the grapevine that I know he's still alive anyway."

Don stopped smiling. "Oh. Sorry, Warren."

And the next day was the day he got expelled from the high school. I thought he might be planning to take off right then and there. "What ya say, Warren, about me headin' South?" he asked me two, three more times. "I dunno," I told him. "Go ask your mother."

I knew damned well he would, too. Dora had a hemorrhage, of course, and I had to listen to her all night.

"Well he's got two whores or something," I says.

She goes pale and says, "two *whats*?" Somehow I figured having two girls instead of just one was less dangerous. If he'd had just one, he might have got her knocked up and have to get married. Seventeen's too young for that. Not in my generation, but in his.

I pulled up at Don's driveway. When he opened the door the cold air blasted in, even without no wind.

"Thanks for the ride, Warren. Sorry if I..."

"You didn't. Night, Don."

When I pulled away, I turned the heater to high, but the noise was so godawful that I had to turn it back down to regular. I wasn't sure whether I wanted to go straight home, or if I didn't maybe want to drive around a little.

I got to thinking about a couple summers ago, when Randolph first brought up the subject of cars.

"You ain't old enough to have a license yet."

"I don't plan to drive it," he says. "I just want to have it here. Some old klunker I can tinker with. Fix it up."

"Fix it up?"

"Oh, you know...new engine and stuff."

"Big V8 with a racing rear-end and a couple of four-barrels?"

He never even smiled. "Something like that."

"You better wait until you can afford all the speeding tickets."

He stood there looking at me and nodding. "So if I was to drive a car into the yard here, you wouldn't let me keep it. Is that right, Warren?"

I knew what he was up to when he said it that way. "That's right. And the same goes for towing or pushing, too."

He grinned right along with me. "You're a hard man, Warren. You want to put that in writing?"

"I can remember," I says. So I went in and sat down in the big bay window so's I could watch and see what he was up to. Sure enough, he takes off up the road with a wheelbarrow and comes back in about fifteen minutes with a front fender. Then the other one five minutes after that. And every time he brought in something new, he'd look up at me there in the window and wave.

I decided not to waste my gas, and I headed to the house. But slow. Main reason I wasn't in a hurry was that Dora had called me about five times that afternoon complaining about Randy. Them two just don't get along. Never did. When Randolph was a toddler, for god's sake, he wouldn't let his own mother pick him up or put him to bed. He'd only let me do that. Odd kid. Always was, and I suppose he always will be odd in one way or another. He started calling me Warren when he was only seven. Said we oughta be friends instead of father and son. I don't believe in this *friend* business. Some people might believe in it, but I don't. A father's a father and a son's a son. I just never have known what to do with him. He can piss me off quicker than anybody I've ever known. But I think it'll all work out once he's grown and he gets over this thing he's got about authority. Personally, I think two years in the army would straighten him out, but he won't hear of it.

I went around a pretty sharp curve and there was the Tennessee Oldsmobile sitting there beside the road. The front end was pulled off far enough, but the ass-end stuck out about half-way into the road. I missed it okay, but if another car been coming, I would have had to take off into the bushes.

I blinked the high beams and looked to see if Randolph was with them, but I couldn't see nobody. I was good and tempted to stop and tell them to get that damn thing off the road before somebody ran into it. I didn't, though, but I kept watching the mirror, even when I couldn't see the car anymore. I couldn't help but wonder if Randolph was there with them.

I was thinking so hard about it and watching the mirror that I didn't see the deer. Then it was too late. I seen the two eyes, wide open and crazy-looking and the body seemed to just follow the eyes out into the road and into the beam of the lights. I swerved off into the weeds, but I didn't miss the deer. The wheel twisted out of my hands when I hit the deer, and the next thing I knew I smacked dead into a tree with this loud crunch, and the radiator blew steam everywhere and made me choke. I just sat there staring at the damn shattered windshield, thinking how much it looked like a cobweb and wondering just where in hell I was.

I don't know how long I sat there like that. Then I noticed the blood drooling down the side of my face from where I'd knocked into the windshield. My head was reeling, and when I tried to get out of the car, I got this shooting pain up my leg. I couldn't figure out what that was from, but when I sat back, the pain wasn't so bad. There I was, only about a half-mile from the house, a dead deer lying there waiting for someone else to come along and hit it, and all I could do was sit there and think about it. The battery was jarred loose and I couldn't blow the horn or flash the lights, and when I tried to holler, it sent this pain all through my back and chest.

The road was dead, dead quiet. We hadn't had hardly any rain that spring, so the gullies along the road were dry and quiet. All I could do was listen and hope someone came along. I started thinking I was seeing things, but from down toward the house I could almost make out the sound of someone coming on foot. Then I heard his whistling. Yessir, I thought. He's on his way to meet his whores. It wasn't long before I could see him. He was carrying a gym bag, and he walked up to the car window like we just ran into each other in a parking lot.

"That you, Warren?" He glanced around and took in the situation.

"None other."

"Jesus, you all right?"

"Not hardly."

"Where's it hurt? Damn, looks like we can start with your head...."

"Can you get that deer out of the road?" I could turn just enough to see it. A buck, not too big. Young. Randolph grabbed it by the horns and tugged and wrestled and negotiated and finally got the thing off the pavement. He was breathing pretty hard when he came to the window again. My leg had started to ache whether I tried to move it or not.

"Where else it hurt?"

"My leg."

He opened the car door. "I guess I'll just have to carry you." He touched my arm real gentle and said, "Arm okay?"

"Yeah."

It took a bit of doing to get me out of the car, and my leg yowled every inch of the way. Finally I was out, sort of balancing on one leg, dizzy like I was going to black out—kind of *wanting* to black out, to tell the truth—and Randolph was trying to figure out the best way to carry me. The whole thing started to seem kind of comical. When my leg wasn't killing me, that is.

"No way in hell you can carry me."

"Well now, you just hold on there a minute, Warren, and we'll see. Here, we can do it this way...."

He bent down and draped me across his shoulders, kind of army style. The jouncing up and down made my head ache, but I figured there wasn't much we could do about it, so I didn't say nothing.

"Seen the Tennessee car up the road just now. Almost hit it."

He didn't say anything. I probably should have just left him alone, but I wanted to hear him say it. "You leaving tonight?"

After a minute he says, "You doing all right up there, Warren?"

"No."

"Think we'll make it?"

"We'll see."

The house was in sight now, but it could have been a mile away for all I knew. My head exploded with every step, and I was ready to just have somebody chop my leg off.

"You mind, Warren?"

"Mind what?"

"If I take off?"

I knew it was best for everybody for him to get away for at least a while, but I went ahead and lied. "Of course I mind."

"That's good," he said.

When we turned into the driveway, I could tell he was getting tired by the way he was staggering. His feet dragged, and he could hardly talk.

"Okay, Warren...I want you...to close your eyes...until we're in the house."

"What the hell for?"

He stopped stock still right there in the driveway and kind of swayed. "I mean it. Close your eyes."

"All right, all right."

I wasn't about to argue at that point, but it did seem strange. It wasn't until two or three weeks later that I remembered that he made me do that. As soon as I closed them, the pain in my leg seemed to die down a little. We went up the steps and into the house. I thought I felt feathers brush against me, but I might have been dreaming. Or delirious. Or maybe I just didn't give a damn.

Henry

I'm looking out the window of my room. Father and Randolph just came home and they were both drunk or something, 'cause Randolph was carrying Father. I can't sleep now, not with Mother screeching and Randolph hollering back at her. Suddenly the porch light comes on, and out comes Randolph. The chicken is still hanging above the door, where he left it a little while ago, but now Randolph takes out a knife and cuts the string. Then he starts walking off up the road, whistling and swinging the chicken around on that string. It makes me wonder who he's going to give it to.

About the author:

Fred Bonnie's published work includes six collections of short stories, the most recent of which is *Detecting Metal*. During his five-year tenure as garden editor of Oxmoor House and *Southern Living Magazine*, he also published six how-to books on gardening.

Fred Bonnie has often set his stories in the workplace, drawing on a varied background to provide material for his fiction. He has, since the age of 11, been a paperboy, caddy, dishwasher, mailroom clerk, book store clerk, short-order cook, milkman, factory worker, busboy, campground custodian, library assistant, professional conversationalist, janitor, bookkeeping supervisor in a bank, country western singer, city directory canvasser, pizza delivery man, horticultural journalist, bartender, advertising and PR executive, caterer, speech writer, chef, and teacher. He currently lives in Columbiana, Alabama, where he makes his living as a free-lance writer.

Fred Bonnie's first novel, *Thanh Ho Delivers*, the story of a Vietnamese immigrant in Birmingham in the 1970s, will be published in the spring of 2000 by Black Belt Press.